VANISHING POINT

The Woman of Porto Pim

The Flying Creatures
of Fra Angelico

Antonio Tabucchi

Vanishing Point

The Woman of Porto Pim
The Flying Creatures of Fra Angelico

Translated from the Italian by
Tim Parks

Chatto & Windus
LONDON

Published in 1991 by
Chatto & Windus
20 Vauxhall Bridge Rd
London SW1V 2SA

The original Italian titles for *Vanishing Point* were *Il filo
dell'orizzonte*; *The Woman of Porto Pim* as *Donna di Porto
Pim* and *The Flying Creatures of Fra Angelico* as *I Volatili
del Beato Angelico*.

Printed in Great Britain by
Mackays of Chatham plc
Chatham, Kent

Contents

Vanishing Point

Author's Note

This book owes much to a city, to a particularly cold winter and to a window. Writing it did not bring me an inordinate amount of levity. All the same I observed that the older one gets the more one tends to laugh on one's own; and that seems to me a step forward towards a more composed and somehow self-sufficient sense of humour.

Spino is a name I invented myself and one I have grown fond of. Some may point out that it's an abbreviation of Spinoza, a philosopher I won't deny I love; but it signifies other things too, of course. Spinoza, let me say in parenthesis, was a Sephardic Jew, and like many of his people carried the horizon with him in his eyes. The horizon, in fact, is a geometrical location, since it moves as we move. I would very much like to think that by some sorcery my character did manage to reach it, since he too had it in his eyes.

A.T.

'Having been' belongs in some way to a 'third kind', radically heterogeneous to both being and non-being.

Vladimir Jankelevitch

To open the drawers you have to turn the handle and press down. This disconnects the spring, the mechanism is set off with a slight metallic click, and the ball bearings automatically begin to slide. The drawers are stacked at a slight angle and run out of their own accord on small rails. First you see the feet, then the stomach, then the chest, then the head of the corpse. Sometimes, when an autopsy hasn't been performed, you have to help the mechanism by pulling the drawer with your hands, since some of the corpses will have bloated stomachs which press against the drawer above and so get stuck. The corpses which have been autopsied on the other hand are dry, as though drained, with a sort of zip fastener along their stomachs and their innards stuffed with sawdust. They make you think of big dolls, large-size puppets from a show whose run has ended, tossed away in a store for old bric-à-brac. And in a way this is life's storehouse. Before their final disappearance, the discarded products of the scene find a last home here while waiting for suitable classification, since the causes of their deaths cannot be left in doubt. That's why they are lying here, and he looks after them and watches over them. He manages the anteroom that leads to the definitive disappearance of their visible image, he records their entry and their departure, he classifies them, he numbers them, sometimes he photographs them, he fills in the file-card that will allow them to vanish from the world of the senses, he hands out their last ticket. He is their last companion, and something more, like a posthumous guardian, impassive and objective.

Then is the distance that separates the living from the dead, he sometimes wonders, really so great? He's unable to answer his own question. In any event cohabitation, if we can call it that, helps to reduce that distance. The corpses have to have a little card attached to their big toes with a registration number, but he's sure that, in the remote way in which they are present, they detest being classified with a number as if they were objects. Because of this, when he thinks about them himself he gives them jokey nicknames, some entirely random, others suggested by a vague likeness to, or circumstance in common with, some character in an old film: Mae West, Professor Unrat, Marcelino Pan y Vino. Pablito Calvo, for example, is the exact double of Marcelino: round face, knobbly knees, a short shiny black fringe. Thirteen years old, Pablito, working illegally, fell off some scaffolding. The father can't be found, the mother lives in Sardinia and can't come. They'll be sending him back to her tomorrow.

(morgue)

Of the original hospital, only the temporary reception ward and the mortuary are still here in this old part of town, otherwise referred to as the historic centre. For a long time now this area has been considered a site for study and restoration. But the years go by, local governments alternate, vested interests change and the part to be restored grows more and more decrepit. And then the city encroaches menacingly from other areas, drawing the attention of the experts elsewhere, to suburbs where the 'productive' population is ever more densely settled, where huge dormitories have been built. It's the buildings in these areas that demand the time of the municipal engineers. Sometimes the hillside will slip, as if it wanted to shrug off those ugly encrustations, and then urgent measures are introduced, special funds made available. Then there are roads to be built, sewers and gas pipes to be linked up, schools, nurseries, clinics. Here in the centre, on the other hand, the agony is diffuse, a slow leprosy that has invaded walls and houses whose decay is stealthy and irreversible, like a death sentence. Here live pensioners, prostitutes, street vendors, fishmongers, unemployed young layabouts, grocers with ancient, damp, dark shops that smell of spices and dried cod, above whose doors one can barely make out faded signs announcing: 'Wines – Colonial Products – Tobaccos'. The dustmen rarely come by; even they disdain the leavings of this second-class humanity. In the evening syringes glitter in the narrow streets,

3

there are plastic bags, the shapeless mass of a dead rat in a corner where a phosphorescent poster put up by the Pest Control Department warns you not to touch the verdigris-coloured bait scattered on the ground.

Sara has frequently said she'd like to come and pick him up those evenings his shift finishes at ten, but he has always forbidden her. Not so much for fear of the people; in the evening the narrow street is home for three quiet prostitutes who have watchful pimps at first-floor windows. No, what worries him most are the bands of rats that roam around aggressively in the evening. Sara has no idea how big they are, he's sure she would be terrified, she can't imagine what they're like. True, the city abounds in rats, but this area has its own special breed. Spino has a theory, but he's never told anyone, least of all Sara. He thinks it's the mortuary that attracts them.

[handwritten marginalia: "contrast to closed metal containers"]

[handwritten marginalia: "no death"]

Saturday evenings they usually go to the Magic Lantern. It's a film club at the top of Vico dei Carbonari in a small courtyard that looks like some corner of a country village, reminds you of farmhouses, patches of countryside, times past. From up here you can see the harbour, the open sea, the tangle of tiny streets in the old Jewish ghetto, the pinkish bell-tower of a church hemmed in between walls and houses, invisible from other parts of the city, unsuspected. You have to climb a brick stairway worn by long use, a long shiny iron bar serving as a handrail, twisting along a pitted wall invaded by tufts of caper plants obscuring faded graffiti. You can still read: 'Long live Coppi', and 'The exploiters' law shall not pass'. Things from years gone by. On summer nights, after the film, they wind up their evening in a small café at the end of the narrow street where two blocks of granite with a chain between them mark off a little terrace complete with pergola and surrounded by a shaky wall. There are four small tables with green iron legs and marble tops where the circles of wine and coffee the marble has absorbed and made its own trace out hieroglyphics, little patterns to interpret, the archaeology of a recent past of other customers, other evenings, drinking bouts perhaps, late nights with card games and singing.

Beneath them the untidy geometry of the city falls sheer away together with the lights of villages along the bay, the world. Sara has a mint granita that they still make here with a primitive little gadget, scraping the ice with a grater fitted inside a small aluminium box where the fragments of frozen water cling together compact and soft as snow. The proprietor is a fat man with bags under his eyes and a lazy walk. He wears a white apron that emphasises his paunch, he smiles, pronounces his always miserable weather predictions: 'Tomorrow it'll get colder, the wind is from the east'; or: 'This haze'll bring rain.' He prides himself on knowing the winds and weather; he was a seaman when he was younger, he worked on a steamship on the Americas route.

Even when it's hot Sara draws in her legs and covers her shoulders with a shawl, since the night air gives her pains in her joints. She looks towards the sea, a brooding mass that might be the night itself were it not for the stationary lights of the ships waiting to come into harbour. 'How nice it would be to get away,' she says, 'wouldn't it?' Sara has been saying how nice it would be to get away for ten years now, and he answers her that one day maybe, sooner or later, they ought to do it. By tacit agreement their exchanges on this subject have never gone beyond these two ritual phrases: yet all the same he knows that Sara dreams of their impossible departure. He knows because it isn't difficult for him to get close to her dreams. There's an ocean liner in her fantasies, with a deckchair under cover and a plaid blanket to protect her from the sea breeze, and some men in white trousers at the end of the deck are playing a game the English play. It takes twenty days to get to South America, but to which city isn't specified: Mar del Plata, Montevideo, Salvador de Bahia, it doesn't matter: South America is small in the space of a dream. It's a film with Myrna Loy that Sara liked a lot: the evenings are stylish, there's dancing on board, the deck is lit up by garlands of lights and the band plays 'What a Night, What a Moon, What a Girl', or some tango from the thirties, like '*Por una cabeza*'. She's wearing an evening dress with a white scarf, she lets the dashing captain flirt with her and waits for her partner to leave the infirmary and come and dance with her. Because, of course, as well as being her partner, Spino is also the ship's doctor.

If Sara's dream is not exactly that, then it's certainly something very like it. The evening they saw *Southern Waters* she looked so wistful; she hugged his arm tight, and while she was eating her granita went back to the old chestnut of his unfinished degree. These days even the line that he is too old doesn't deter her. Won't she accept, he says, once and for all, that at his age you don't feel like going back to school any more? And then the university registration book, the bureaucracy, his old college friends who would be his examiners now. It would be intolerable. But it's no good, she doesn't give up: life is long, she says, longer maybe than one expects, and you don't have the right to throw it away. At which he prefers to look off into the distance, doesn't answer, falls silent to let the matter drop and to avoid it leading to another argument that's connected to his not getting his degree. It's a subject that distresses him, this: he understands well enough how she feels about it, but what can he do? Of course at their age this life as secret lovers is a somewhat inconvenient eccentricity, but it's so difficult to break with old habits, to pass suddenly into married life. And then, the idea of becoming the father of that evasive eighteen-year-old with his absurd way of speaking and indolent, slovenly manner terrifies him. Sometimes he sees the boy walk by on his way back from school and thinks: I would be your father, your substitute father.

No, this is definitely not something he wants to talk about. But Sara doesn't want to talk about it either; she wants him to want to. So like him she doesn't mention it; instead she talks about films. The Magic Lantern has been holding two retrospectives dedicated to Myrna Loy and Humphrey Bogart; they even showed *Strictly Confidential*: there's more than enough for them to chew over here. Did he notice the scarves Myrna Loy was wearing? Of course he did, for heaven's sake, they're so flashy; but Bogart's foulards as well, always so fluffy and with those polkadots, truly unbearable . . . sometimes it seems like wafts of cologne and Brylcreem are coming off the screen. Sara laughs quietly, with that delicate way of catching her breath she has. But why don't they have a retrospective for Virginia Mayo, too? That Bogart treated her like a dog, the bastard. She has a special soft spot for Virginia Mayo, who died in a motel room, destroyed by alcohol, because he'd dropped her. But, *by the way*, that ship in the harbour, doesn't it look like a liner? It has too many lights, she thinks, to be a cargo ship. He isn't sure, hmm, no, he wouldn't know. Though perhaps, no, they don't have ocean liners any more these days, they're all in the breakers' yards, just a few left for cruises. People travel by plane these days, who would cross the Atlantic in a liner? She says: 'Right, you're right,' but he senses from her tone that she doesn't agree, is merely resigned. Meanwhile the proprietor of the café moves around with a cloth in his hand, wiping the empty tables. It's a silent message: if they would be so kind as to call it a day he could close down and get off to bed, he's been on his feet since eight this morning and the years weigh heavier than his paunch. Then the breeze has got a bit fresh, the night is oppressively silent and humid, you can feel a film of brine on the arms of the chairs, perhaps they really had better go. Sara agrees it would be better. Her eyes are bright, he never knows whether this is emotion or mere tiredness.

'I'd like you to sleep with me tonight,' she tells him. Spino says he'd like to as well. But tomorrow is his day off, she'll come to his place in the morning and they'll be together until evening. He'll prepare a quick snack to eat in the kitchen and they can spend the whole afternoon in bed. She whispers what a shame it is they met so late in life, when everything was already settled; she's sure she would have been happy with him. Perhaps he's thinking the same thing, but to cheer her up he tells her no, it's one thing being lovers and quite another being married, the daily routine is love's worst enemy, it grinds it down.

The proprietor of the café is already lowering his shutters and mumbles goodnight under his breath.

death

They brought him in in the middle of the night. The ambulance arrived quietly, its lights dipped, and Spino immediately thought: something horrific has happened. He had the impression he'd been asleep and yet he picked up the sound of the ambulance's motor perfectly clearly, heard it turn into the narrow street too calmly, as if there were nothing more that could be done, and he sensed how death arrives slowly, how that is death's real pace, unhurried and inexorable.

At this time of night the city is asleep, this city which never rests during the day. The noise of the traffic dies down, just every now and then the lonely roar of a truck from along the coast road. Through the empty expanses of night-time silence comes the hum of the steelworks that stands guard over the town to the west, like some ghostly sentinel with lunar lighting. The doors of the ambulance echoed wearily in the courtyard, then he heard the sliding door open and felt he was picking up that smell the night's freshness leaves in people's clothes, not unlike the sour, slightly unpleasant smell some rooms have when they've been slept in. There were four policemen, their faces ashen, four boys with dark hair and the movements of sleepwalkers. They said nothing. A fifth had stayed outside and stammered something in the dark that Spino couldn't catch. At which the four went out, moving as though they didn't really know what they were doing. He had the impression of witnessing a graceful, funereal ballet whose choreography he couldn't understand.

Then they came in again with a corpse on a stretcher. Everything was done in silence. They shifted the corpse from the stretcher and Spino laid it out on the stainless-steel slab. He opened the stiffened hands, tied the jaws tight with a bandage. He didn't ask anything, because everything was only too clear, and what did the mere mechanics of the facts matter? He recorded the time of arrival in the register and pushed the bell that rang on the first floor to get the doctor on duty to come and certify death. The four boys sat down on the enamelled bench and smoked. They seemed shipwrecked. Then the doctor came down and started to talk and write. He looked at the fifth boy, who was wounded and was moaning softly. Spino telephoned the New Hospital and told them to prepare the operating theatre for an urgent case, then immediately arranged for the boy to be sent there. 'We haven't even got any instruments here,' he said. 'We're just a mortuary now.'

The doctor went out by the back stairs and

someone, one of the boys, sobbed, and murmured: 'Mother,' pushing his hands into his eyes, as if to erase a scene that had been etched there. At which Spino felt an oppressive tiredness, as though the exhaustion of everything around him were bearing down on his shoulders. He went outside and sensed that even the courtyard was tired, and the walls of this old hospital were tired, the windows too, and the city, and everything. He looked up and had the impression that even the stars were tired, and he wished there were some escape from this universal tiredness, some kind of postponement or forgetting.

4

He walked all morning by the harbour. He got as far as the Customs and the cargo docks. There was an ugly ship with 'Liberia' written on the poop, unloading bags and boxes. A black leaning against the guardrail watching the unloading procedure waved to him and he waved back. Then a thick bank of low cloud rose from the sea and only moments later had reached the shore, wrapping itself round the lighthouse and the derricks, which dissolved in fog. The harbour grew dark and the iron structures shiny. He crossed the Piazza delle Vettovaglie and went to the elevator cars that go up to the hills beyond the frame of the apartment blocks that form a bastion around the city. There was no one on the cars now, they fill up in the late afternoon when people come home from work. The operator is a little old man with a smoke-dark suit and a wooden hand. On his lapel he wears a war invalid's badge. He's extremely efficient at using his one good hand to operate the levers and that strange iron ring that looks like the controls of a tram. Alongside the windows of the cabin, which in this first stretch of the journey runs on rails like a funicular, blank walls of houses march by, interrupted by small dark openings inhabited by cats, gates leading through to courtyards where you can glimpse a little washbowl, a rusty bicycle, geraniums and basil planted in tuna tins. Then all at once the walls open up: it's as if the car had burst through the roofs and was headed straight for the sky. For a moment you feel you're hanging in the void, the traction cables slide silently, the harbour and the buildings fall rapidly away below, you almost have the impression that the lifting movement will never stop, the law of gravity seems an absurdity and the town a toy it's a relief to be leaving behind you.

You stop at the edge of a meagre garden with a shelter. It's like a railway station in the mountains, there's even a wooden seat cut from a tree trunk. If you didn't turn to look at the sea you could think you were in Switzerland or on the hills above some German lake. From here there's a path that leads away to a Hungarian trattoria. That's its name, 'Hungary', and inside there's a handsome old woman and her irritable husband. The customers speak a hesitant Italian and argue amongst themselves in Hungarian. Heaven knows why they insist on keeping this poor shack open. Every time Spino goes the place is deserted; the old woman is solicitous and calls him Captain, it's ridiculous, she has always called him Captain.

He sat down at a table near the window, it's incredible how at this height the sound of the ships' sirens is clearer than down below. He ordered lunch and then a coffee that the woman always prepares Turkish style, serving it up in huge blue porcelain cups that belong perhaps to her Hungarian youth.

After the meal he rested a while, his eyes open, head on his hands, but noticing nothing, exactly as if he were sleeping. He sat there listening to time slipping slowly by; the cuckoo in the clock over the kitchen door popped out and cuckooed five times. The old woman arrived and brought him a teapot wrapped in a felt cloth. He sipped tea for a long time. The old man was playing patience at the next table and every now and then looked up at him, screwing his eyes into a smile as he indicated the cards that wouldn't come out. He invited Spino to join him and they played a game of *briscola*, both concentrating on the cards as if they were the most important thing in the world, as if upon them depended the outcome of some event which remained obscure, but which they both sensed was superior to the reality of their own presence here. Dusk fell pale blue and the old woman turned on the lights behind the counter, two parchment lampshades spotted with fly droppings and supported by two stuffed squirrels, somewhat absurd in a trattoria that looks out over a seaport.

So then he telephoned Corrado, but he wasn't in the editorial office. They managed to track him down in Typesetting. He seemed rather excited. 'But where have you been?' he shouted, to make himself heard over the noise of the machines, 'I've been trying to get you all day.' Spino told him he was in the Hungary; if Corrado wanted to come and meet him there he'd be happy to see him. He was on his own. Corrado told him he couldn't, and his tone seemed brusque, perhaps annoyed. He explained that they were about to start printing the paper and the crime page read like a boring official report, that squalid story the whole city would be reading about tomorrow. He'd been trying to reconstruct what had happened all day without managing to put together a decent article. The reporter he'd sent out to the scene had come back with a garbled version. Nobody knew anything and asking at the police station was worse than trying to see in the dark. If only he'd been able to find Spino a bit earlier he could have asked him for a couple of details. He'd heard he'd been on duty. 'They didn't even want to tell me his name,' he finished, huffily. 'All I know is that he had false papers.'

Spino said nothing, and Corrado calmed down. From the receiver Spino heard the noise of the machines working rhythmically with a liquid sound, like waves. 'You come over here,' Corrado began again, suddenly disarming, 'please,' and Spino seemed to see the childish expression Corrado's face has when he's upset.

'I can't,' he said. 'I'm sorry, Corrado, but this evening I really can't. I'll call you back tomorrow maybe, or the day after.'

'Okay,' Corrado said, 'I wouldn't have time to change the piece now anyway. All I need is his name. You didn't hear anything, last night? Do you remember if someone mentioned a name?'

Spino looked out of the window. Night had fallen and a waterfall of lights was spilling down the hillside, cars driving into town. He thought for a moment about the previous night, re-membering nothing. Odd, the only image that came to mind was a stagecoach in an old film; it shot out from the right-hand side of the screen, growing enormous as it came into close-up, as if heading straight for him, a child watching its approach in the front row of the Aurora cinema. There was a masked rider galloping after it. Then the guard tucked his rifle into his shoulder and the screen exploded with a crashing shot as Spino covered his eyes.

'Call him The Kid,' he said.

5

The article in the *Gazzetta del Mare* was unsigned, a brief note on the front page leading the reader to the Home News section, where the story took up two columns: a modest space on an inside page. To compensate, there was a photograph of the dead man. It's the photo the police took. Corrado managed to get them to give it to him, and anyhow, if they want to find out who the man is, it suits the police to have it published. Under the photo they've put the caption: 'Gunman Without a Name.'

He opened the paper on the table, pushing aside the breakfast things, while Sara began to tidy up the other rooms. 'See?' she shouted from the kitchen. 'Seems nobody knows him. But the article can't be by Corrado, it isn't even signed.'

Spino knows it's not by Corrado. The facts were dug up by a young and very enterprising reporter who a few months ago caused pandemonium when he wrote on corruption at the docks. Spino sticks to the main story, skipping the opening paragraph about the fight against crime, full of clichés.

A tragic gun battle took place last night in the working-class Arsenale district in a flat on the top floor of an old block in Via Casedipinte. Acting on a tip-off from a source which police are keeping strictly secret, five men of the Police Special Corps raided the flat shortly after midnight. At the warning, 'Open up! Police!' an unspecified number of persons in the flat fired repeatedly through the door, seriously wounding one policeman, Antonino di Nola, 26, who has been stationed in our city for only two months. Di Nola later underwent what was described as delicate surgery. After the shooting, the gunmen barricaded themselves in a small room leading off from the entrance hall before escaping from a window across the rooftops. But before fleeing (and this perhaps is the most obscure part of the whole incident) they shot one of their own gang. The man was raced to the Old Hospital but was dead on arrival. His identity is unknown. It appears he was carrying false documents. Between twenty and twenty-five years old, brown beard, blue eyes, slim, of average height, to all intents and purposes the dead man was a stranger to local inhabitants, despite having lived in the area for about a year. He went under the name of Carlo Noboldi and claimed to be a student, although enquiries made at university offices have revealed that he was not enrolled. Shopkeepers in the area say he was courteous and polite and always paid his bills on time. The flat, which has two rooms and a loft, belongs to a religious order which took Noboldi in last year when he claimed he had just returned from abroad and was out of money. The Prior of the Order, to which Noboldi was paying a nominal rent, declined to make any statement to journalists. This murder, which once again sees our city as the stage for violent crime, will intensify the fears of a population already deeply disturbed by recent events.

Sara has now come up behind him and, leaning over his shoulder, starts to read the paper, her head beside his. She passes a hand through his hair, a gesture of understanding and tenderness. For a moment, engrossed, they stare at the photograph of the unidentified man. Then she lets slip a remark that leaves him shaken: 'Grow a beard and lose twenty years and it could be you.'

He doesn't reply, as if this observation were of no importance.

6

On the sliding door Pasquale had left a note:
'Back Soon'. Pasquale always goes and has
his morning coffee around eleven. Instead of
waiting in the courtyard, Spino decided to go and
join him, after all he knew where to find him. The
sun was bright, the streets were pleasant. He went
out of the hospital and down a dark side street
that led into a small square where there was a café
with a terrace and tables laid out. Pasquale was
sitting at a table reading the paper. Spino must
have frightened him, because when he came up
from behind and spoke to him, Pasquale started
slightly. With a look of resignation he folded his
paper and left some money on the table. They
walked along calmly, as if out for a stroll. Then
Pasquale said it was a sad story, to which Spino
replied, 'Right,' and Pasquale said: 'I want to be
buried in my own village. That's where I want
them to put me, beneath the mountains.'

A bus went by and the noise drowned out their
last words. They crossed a patch of garden where
people had worn a footpath between flowerbeds
defended by 'Keep Off' signs. Spino said he
wasn't going to the morgue, he just wanted to

know if anybody had shown up, a relative, someone who knew the man. Pasquale shook his head with an expression of disgust and said: 'What a world.' Spino asked him not to leave the morgue if he could possibly avoid it, and Pasquale replied that if the relatives did come forward, the first place they'd go would be to the police, they certainly wouldn't come to the hospital. They parted at the crossroads where the path through the gardens plunges between the houses of the old city centre, and Spino set off to catch the number 37.

Corrado wasn't in the office, as Spino had feared. He had guessed his friend would want to go in person to try and find out more. Obviously the facts his reporter had picked up hadn't satisfied him. He hung around in the editorial office for a while, saying hello to people he knew, but no one paid much attention to him. There was an atmosphere of impatience and nervous tension, and Spino imagined that this death with its burden of tragedy was weighing down on the room, making the men feel feverish and vulnerable. Then somebody came through a door waving a piece of paper and shouting that the tanks had crossed the frontiers, and he named a city in Asia, some improbable place. And shortly afterwards another journalist working at a teleprinter went over to a colleague and told him that the agreements had been signed, and he mentioned another distant foreign city, something feasible perhaps out there in Africa, but as unlikely-sounding here as the first. And Spino realised that the dead man he was thinking of meant nothing to anybody; it was one small death in the huge belly of the world, an insignificant corpse with no name and no history, a waste fragment of the architecture of things, a scrap-end. And while he was taking this in, the noise in that modern room full of machines suddenly stopped, as if his understanding had turned a switch reducing voices and gestures to silence. And in this silence he had the sensation of moving like a fish caught in a net; his body made a sudden involuntary jerk and his hand knocked an empty coffee cup off a table. The sound of the cup breaking on the floor started up the noise in the room again. Spino apologised to the owner of the cup, who smiled as if to say it didn't matter, and Spino left.

7

'Still No Name for the Victim of Via Case-dipinte.' It's the headline of an article by Corrado. His initials are at the bottom. It's a resigned, tired piece, full of clichés: the police search, all leads meticulously followed up, the enquiry at a dead end.

Spino noticed the involuntary irony: a dead end. He reflects that one person is definitely dead and no one knows who he is, so much so that they can't even legally declare him dead. There's just the corpse of a young man with a thick beard and a sharp nose. Spino starts to use his imagination. He was dead on arrival at the hospital, but perhaps in the ambulance he mumbled something: cursed, begged, mentioned a name. Perhaps he called for his mother, as is only natural, or for a wife, or child. He could have children. He is married. There's a ring on his finger, always given that it is his ring. But of course it's his. No one wears somebody else's ring.

But no, says Corrado in his article. He didn't say anything while he was being driven to the hospital, he was in a coma, to all intents and

25

purposes already dead. The policemen involved in the shoot-out said so.

Spino found a pen and underlined the parts he thought most interesting.

His photograph has been sent to every police station in Italy, but there appears to be no trace of him in police files . . . It is believed that if he had been a member of an underground organisation, his comrades would have made some kind of announcement by now . . . As things stand at the moment police cannot be sure that the young man was a terrorist . . . What's more, according to informed sources, the tip-off given to the police could be part of an underworld or perhaps mafia vendetta . . . The identity-card found on the murdered man belongs to Mr I.F. of Turin, who lost it two years ago and reported the loss in the regular fashion . . . And lastly there is the curious detail of the name on the door. Written on a plastic strip, the kind of thing anyone can print out themselves with a Dyno machine, it says: Carlo Nobodi (not 'Noboldi', as we mistakenly reported yesterday). The name is obviously false, a perhaps significant adaptation of the English word 'nobody'.

Suddenly he thought of the ring. He telephoned the mortuary and Pasquale's voice answered.

'Has he still got his ring on?'

'Who is it? Can I help you?'

'It's Spino. I want to know if he's still got his ring on.'

'What ring? What are you talking about?'

'Doesn't matter,' said Spino. 'I'll be right over.'

*

'Nobody shown up?' Spino asks him.

Pasquale shakes his head and lifts his eyes to the ceiling with a resigned expression, as if to say that the corpse will have to stay where it is. The clothes are in the locker, the forensic people have left them there because they didn't consider them important. They didn't even bother to search through them carefully, otherwise they'd have found a photograph in his breast pocket. Pasquale points to it, he's put it under the glass top on the desk. It's a snap from a contact sheet, about as big as a postage stamp. It must be an old photo, in any event he ought to hand it over to the policeman on duty, it's compulsory. But the policeman's not there at the moment. He was there half the morning and then they called him out for something urgent. He's a young lad who does patrolwork as well.

Spino had expected to have trouble with the ring, but in the event it slips off easily. The hands aren't swollen and then the ring seems too big for the finger. On the inside, as he was hoping, there's a name and a date: 'Pietro, 12.4.1939'. Pasquale is surprised out of his sleepiness and comes over to take a look. Chewing a toffee, he mutters something incomprehensible. Spino shows him the ring and he looks at his friend inquisitively.

'But what are you after?' Pasquale says in a whisper. 'Why are you so bothered about finding out who he is?'

8

They got on the bus in Piazza del Parlasolo, under the bell-tower. The clock said eight o'clock, and, it being Sunday, the square was quiet, deserted almost, the three buses lined up in a row, their engines ticking over, each with a card on its windscreen announcing a destination. The clock struck eight and the driver promptly folded up his paper, pressed a button to close the automatic doors and slipped into gear. They went to sit up front, on the driver's side, Sara by the window. On the seat at the back was a group of Boy Scouts, halfway down the aisle an elderly couple in Sunday best, then themselves.

Sara had brought sandwiches and on her knees held a guidebook to Romanesque churches in the area. The book was in colour and its cover featured a stone ceiling rose. The bus drove along the almost deserted sea front. The traffic lights hadn't been switched on yet and the driver slowed down at every intersection. After the flower market they took a wide road that climbed rapidly in long curves. In just a few minutes they were halfway up the hillside, already out of town, running along beside an old ruined aqueduct.

Another moment and it was open country with thickets of trees and vegetable gardens planted on terraces; olive, acacia and mimosa trees seemed on the point of flowering despite the season. Below, they looked down to the sea and the coast, both pale blue and veiled in a light mist which didn't penetrate the city itself.

Sara closed her eyes and slept a little perhaps. Spino's eyes were also half-closed as he let himself be lulled by the motion of the bus. The Boy Scouts got off a stop before the village by a roadside Madonna. Then the bus crossed the village and turned round in the square, stopping in a yellow rectangle painted on the flagstones. Before starting their climb they had a coffee in a milk-bar in the square. The little woman behind the counter watched them with a curiosity they satisfied by asking for directions to the sanctuary. She spoke in a harsh, rather primitive dialect, showing bad teeth. They gathered she was suggesting they eat in a trattoria that belonged to her daughter where the cooking was good and the prices reasonable.

They decided instead to climb up the path marked in their guide. The book promised a steep but picturesque walk with dramatic views across the bay and the countryside inland. All of a sudden the bell-tower rose pink and white amongst the holm oaks. Sara took Spino by the hand, pulling him along, like two children coming out of school.

The churchyard is paved with stone flags, grass growing in the cracks between, while a low brick wall runs along the edge of a sheer drop to the other side. From up here the horizon stretches away from one bay to the next and the sea breeze blows in with a sharp tang. On the façade, near the door, an inscription explains how in the year of grace MCCCXXV the Madonna now in the sanctuary was carried in procession down to the sea, where she vanquished the terrible plague then afflicting the valley, after which the people chose the Madonna as patron saint of the bay. The first stone of the convent annex was laid on 12 June MCCCXXV and the inscription preserves the memory of that day. Sara read aloud from her guidebook, insisting that Spino pay attention.

The sun was hot. To eat their sandwiches they stretched out on a patch of grass at the end of the churchyard where an iron cross on a stone pedestal commemorates a solemn visit paid by the Bishop in 1918, in gratitude, it says, for the end of the war, and for Victory. They ate slowly and calmly, enjoying the pleasure of being there, and when the sun began to slip behind the promontory, leaving a hazy light along the coast, they went into the church by a side door near the apse where a fresco shows a knight on a white horse crossing a landscape dominated by a naive allegorical representation with a background of spring celebrations and festivals to the left and fires and hangings to the right. Then they went around the aisles, looking at the votive paintings hung on the walls. Most of them show sea scenes: shipwrecks, miraculous visions saving mariners from storms, windjammers, their rigging devastated by lightning, finding the right route thanks to the intercession of the Madonna. The Holy Mother is always shown between flashing clouds, her head covered by an azure veil as in popular iconography, her right hand reaching through the sky to make a gesture of protection toward the wave-tossed boats. Crude handwriting has traced out phrases of devotion across the paint.

Then the bell rang out and the Prior came in from the vestry to celebrate afternoon Mass. They sat to one side, near the confession-box, reading the inscriptions on the stone slabs on the walls. Afterwards, they found the Prior in the vestry as he was taking off his vestments and he led them through to his study next to the now empty cells of the convent beyond the refectory. Perhaps he mistook them for a mature married couple wanting advice, who knows, or for two inquisitive tourists. He invited them to sit on a small couch in a bare room: there was a dark table, a small organ, a bookcase with glass doors. On that table, with a chestnut leaf to mark his place, was a book about destiny and tarot. So then Spino said he had come about a man who had died, and the priest immediately understood and asked if they were relatives or friends of the man. Neither, he said, the first time he'd seen him he was already dead, and now he was being kept in a refrigerator, like a fish, but he ought to be given a proper burial. The priest nodded in agreement, since from his piont of view he imagined he was hearing, and perhaps in the

31

words of another was warming to, a version of his own compassion as a man of faith. But what could he say? Yes, he had known the boy, but not in the sense of knowing his name, place of birth and so on. He had always believed he was called Carlo and perhaps he really was. All he could say about him was that he was a nice boy, he loved his studies, he had said he was poor, the Order had helped him. He didn't know for certain if he was really born in Argentina, that was what he had said, and the Prior had never doubted it, and why should he have? In the two months he had stayed in the monastery he had read a great deal and they had talked a great deal. Then he had moved to town so as to be able to study and the Order had continued to help him by offering the modest charity of a low rent. He was sorry he had gone, he was a boy with a sharp, clear mind.

He looked them in the eyes, insistently, as priests will sometimes. 'Why do you want to know about him?' he asked.

'Because he is dead and I'm alive,' Spino said.

He wasn't sure why he'd answered like that. He felt it was the only plausible answer, since, truth to tell, there was no other reason. So then the priest clasped his hands together on the table, and stretching out his arms his white cassock slipped back to show his wrists, which were also white, and his fingers fidgeted a little with each other.

'He wrote to me,' said the priest. 'I'll show you the letter.' He opened a drawer and took out a blue envelope with a postcard inside showing a view of the city that Spino sees every day. The priest handed it to him and he read the few lines written there in a large, rather childish hand. Then Spino asked if anyone else had seen it, and the priest shook his head smiling, as if to say that no one had bothered to come and talk to him. 'I couldn't be of much use to the police,' he said, 'and then it's too much of an effort to climb up here.'

They exchanged a few casual remarks about the beauty of the place and the history of the church. Sara embarked on a pleasant conversation with the priest about the frescoes, Spino restricting himself to listening to their authoritative remarks as they spoke easily about the Knight, the Angel, Death, the Hanged Man; until he remarked that it was odd but they sounded like tarot figures, and he pointed to the book on the table. 'I wouldn't have thought you'd like it, Father,' he added, 'it being about life's strange coincidences.'

The priest smiled and looked at him indulgently. 'Only God knows all the coincidences of this existence, but it is we alone who must choose our own set of coincidences from all those possible,' he said, 'we alone.' And so saying he pushed the book towards Spino.

So then, for fun, Spino took the book and opened it at random without looking. He said: 'Page forty-six,' and with a solemn voice, as if pretending to be a fortune teller, read out the first paragraph. They laughed out of politeness, as one does after an amusing remark, and it was clear that this laughter also marked the end of their conversation. So they said goodbye and the priest showed them out. The sky was growing dark and they hurried down the path having heard the horn of the bus in the village square announcing its imminent departure.

Sara flopped on her seat with a sigh of satisfaction and tidied her hair slyly. 'We should go on holiday,' she said. 'We need a holiday.' He nodded without saying anything and leaned his head back on the headrest. The driver turned off the interior lights and the bus sped out of the village and along the hillside. Spino closed his eyes and thought of destiny, of the sentence he had read from that book, of life's infinite coincidences. And when he opened them again the bus was already driving through the pitch dark and Sara had gone to sleep with her head on his shoulder.

9

Seeing him holed away behind his desk with that childish frown he sometimes had when he'd got too much to do, Spino thought how as always Corrado loved to play the part of the cynical press editor, a type they've seen together at the cinema so many times. Spino had arrived ready to tell his friend about his Sunday outing. The morning's newspaper, as always on Mondays, was almost exclusively given over to football and contained no news of any importance. He would have liked to have told Corrado that Sara was perhaps about to set off for a short holiday, and if he wanted to take him on free of charge as a private investigator, here was an occasion not to be missed.

But when Corrado said: 'Another,' making a two sign with his fingers, Spino's good humour suddenly evaporated and he sat down without the courage to speak, waiting.

'The policeman died last night,' Corrado said, and he made a gesture with his hand, a cutting gesture, as if to say: quits; or perhaps: end of story. There was a long silence and Corrado began to leaf through the pages of a file as if there was nothing more to say about the matter. Then he took off his glasses and said calmly: 'The funeral will be held tomorrow, the corpse is laid out in a mortuary room at the police barracks, the press agencies have already released the text of the official telegrams of condolence.' He put the file back on a shelf and fed a piece of paper into his typewriter. 'I've got to write it up,' he said. 'I'm doing it myself because I don't want any trouble, just straightforward news, no speculation, no fancy stuff.'

He made as if to start writing, but Spino put a hand on the machine. 'Listen, Corrado,' he said, 'yesterday I spoke to a priest who knew him, I saw a letter. He was a sensitive person, maybe this business isn't so simple as it seems.'

Corrado jumped to his feet, went to the door of his little glass office and closed it. 'Oh, he was sensitive, was he?' he exclaimed, turning red. Spino didn't answer. He shook his head in a sign of denial, as if not understanding. So then Corrado said to listen very carefully, because there were only two possible explanations. First: that when the police arrived the dead man was already dead. In fact the Kid died by the door to the apartment. Now the gun that killed both him and the policeman, from which six shots were fired, was found on the kitchen balcony at the end of a short passage. So obviously it wasn't suicide since a dead man couldn't possibly run back the whole length of the passage and go out on the balcony to leave the gun there. Second explanation: the gun, with somebody holding it, was on the balcony, waiting. The Kid knew this, or didn't know, impossible to be sure. At a certain point the police knock on the door and the Kid calmly goes to open it. And at that moment the gun pokes in from the night and fires repeatedly both on the Kid and on the police. So then, who was the dead man? An unknowing bait? Or aware that he was a bait? A poor fool? Someone who wasn't involved at all? An inconvenient witness? Or something else again? All hypotheses were possible. Was it terrorism? Perhaps. But it could equally well have been something else: vendettas, fraud, something secret, blackmail, who knows. Perhaps the Kid was the key to everything, but he might also have been just a sacrificial victim, or someone who stumbled into an encounter with destiny. Only one thing Corrado was sure of: that it was best to forget the whole business.

'But you can't let people die in a vacuum,' Spino said. 'It's as if they'd died twice over.'

Corrado got up and took his friend by the arm, pulling him gently to the door. He made an impatient gesture, pointing to the clock on the wall. 'What do you think you're going to find out?' he said, pushing him outside.

rhetorical questions

Terroism

10

'Indian summer St Martin's Day, winter can't be far away.' Somebody used to say that to him when he was a boy, and in vain Spino struggled to remember who it was. He thought about it on a station platform swept by cold gusts of wind, waving as the train bellied out into the curve. He also thought that a lot could happen in three days. And in his mind a childish voice was laughing, saying: 'Three little orphans! Three little orphans!' It was a piercing, malignant voice, but one he couldn't recognise, recovered from some distant past when memory had stored away the emotion but not the event that produced it. Leaving the station he turned to look at the lighted clockface on the façade and said to himself: Tomorrow is another day.

Sara had gone on holiday. Her school had organised a three-day trip to Lake Maggiore and Spino encouraged her to go. He asked her to send him some postcards from Duino and she smiled with complicity. If they had had some time they would have talked about it: once they talked a lot about Rilke; and now he would have liked to talk about a poem that takes as its subject a photograph of the poet's father, something he's been repeating to himself by heart all day.

At home he set up his instruments in the kitchen where there was more space to work than in the cubby-hole he normally used as his dark-room. In the afternoon he had picked up a supply of reagent and bought a plastic bowl in the gardening department of a big store. He arranged the paper on the dining table, setting the stand on the enlarger at maximum. He got a frame of light thirty centimetres by forty and inserted the negative of the contact photo which he'd had rephotographed in a lab where he knows he can trust people.

He printed the whole photograph, leaving the enlarger on a few seconds more than necessary since the contact shot was overexposed. In the bowl of reagent the outline appeared to be struggling to emerge, as if a distant reality, past now, irrevocable, were reluctant to be resurrec-ted, were resisting the profanation of curious, foreign eyes, this awakening in a context to which it didn't belong. That family group, he sensed, was refusing to come back and exhibit itself in this theatre of images he'd set up, refusing to satisfy the curiosity of a stranger in a strange place and in a time no longer its own. He realised too that he was evoking ghosts, trying to extort from them, through the ignoble stratagem of chemistry, a forced complicity, an ambiguous compromise that they had unknowingly under-written with an unguarded pose delivered up to a photographer of long ago. Oh, the questionable virtue of the quick snap! They're smiling. And that smile is for him now, even if they don't like it. The intimacy of an unrepeatable instant of their lives is his now, stretched out across the years, always identical to itself, visible an infinite number of times, hung dripping on a string that crosses his kitchen. A scratch that the process has enlarged out of all proportion slashes diagonally across their bodies and their surroundings. Is it an unintentional fingernail scratch, the inevitable wear and tear things get, the scratch of a piece of metal perhaps (keys, watch, a lighter), something those faces have shared a pocket or drawer with? Or was it done intentionally, the work of a hand that wanted to destroy that past? But that past, like it or not, is part of another present now, offers itself up, despite itself, for interpretation. It shows the veranda of a modest suburban house, stone steps, a scrubby climbing plant with pale bell-shaped flowers twisting round the architrave. It must be summer. The light seems dazzling and the people photographed are wearing summer clothes. The man's face has a surprised and at the same time lethargic expression. He's wearing a white shirt, sleeves rolled up, and is sitting behind a small marble table. In front of him on the table is a glass jug with a folded newspaper propped against it. Obviously he was reading when the unexpected photographer said something to get him to look up. The mother is coming out of the door, she only just gets into the frame and doesn't even realise. She has a short apron with a flower pattern, her face is thin. She's still young, but her youth seems over. The two children are sitting on a step, but apart, strangers to each other. The girl has pigtails bleached by the sun, spectacles rimmed with plastic, clogs. In her lap she holds a rag doll. The boy is wearing sandals and short trousers. He's got his elbows on his knees, his chin on his hands. His face is round, his hair has a few glossy curls, his knees are dirty. Sticking out of his pocket is the fork of a catapult. He's looking straight ahead, but his eyes are lost beyond the lens, as if he were watching some apparition in the air, some event of which the other people in the photograph are unaware. He's looking slightly upwards too, the pupils betray the fact, no doubt about it. Perhaps he's looking at a cloud, at the top of a tree. In the right-hand corner, where the space opens into a stone-flagged lane over which the roof of the veranda is tracing a staircase of shadow, you can just see the curled-up body of a dog. Not interested in the animal, the photographer has caught it in the frame by accident, but left out its head. It's a small dog with mottled black fur, something like a fox terrier, but definitely a mongrel.

There's something that disturbs him in this peaceful snap of nameless people, something that seems to be escaping his interpretation, a hidden signal, an apparently insignificant element which nevertheless he senses is crucial. Then he moves in closer, his attention caught by a detail. Through the glass of the jug, distorted by the water, the letters on the folded newspaper the man has before him spell: *Sur.* Realising he's getting excited, he says to himself: Argentina, we're in Argentina. Why am I getting excited? What's Argentina got to do with it? But now he knows what the boy's eyes are staring at. Behind the photographer, immersed in the foliage, is a pink and white country villa. The boy is staring at a window where the shutters are closed, because that shutter could slowly open just a crack, and then . . .

And then what? Why is he dreaming up this story? What is this his imagination is inventing and trying to palm off as memory? But just then, not inventing, but really hearing it in his mind, a child's voice distinctly calls: 'Biscuit! Biscuit!' Biscuit is the name of a dog, it can't be otherwise.

11

When you reach the top of Via della Salita Vecchia the town thins out into the hinterland, settles down into a dull plain that the ramparts of the hills would never have led you to suspect. Here the lava-flow of cement hasn't arrived yet and buildings put up in the twenties, the ones the bombs spared, are still standing: small villas built in a fanciful, petit-bourgeois *déco* which, over the years, time's patina has managed one way or another to ennoble; and then more modest houses, surrounded by walls and vegetable patches, with a few tufts of yellow reeds near the fences, as though this were already the country. The main road is lined by two rows of identical two-storey terraced houses with outside brick staircases and tiny windows. They were put up under Fascism. This area was planned as a residential suburb for the clerical staffs of municipal boards, the bureaucrats, members of the less important professions. What the place has preserved of that period and world is the formality, the sadness. Yet there is something charming in the landscape: there's a small square with a fountain, some flowerbeds, a few rusty swings, a bench where two old ladies with their shopping bags are chatting. And this meagre, inert charm makes the place feel almost unreal: as likewise improbable, perhaps non-existent, is the thing he is looking for. *F. Poerio, Tailor, Via Cadorna 15.* That's what the telephone directory says. The dead man's jacket is an old tweed with leather patches on the elbows. It could be ten years old, maybe fifteen. It's too insignificant a clue to lead to anything. And then who knows whether it's the same tailor. Perhaps there are other Poerios working as tailors in other cities in Italy.

And meanwhile he walks along Via R. Cadorna, a narrow avenue lined with lime trees. The houses here are small, detached, two-storey villas preserving vestiges of the wealth of a bygone age. Many of them could do with a fresh coat of paint on walls and shutters, their scanty gardens show signs of neglect and washing has been hung out to dry from some of the windows. Number fifteen is a house with a wrought-iron fence which has been taken over by wild ivies. The entrance is sheltered by a little porch, likewise wrought-iron and of vaguely oriental design. A glass nameplate says: *Poerio, Tailor.* The letters, once gold, are sandy now and spotted with little stains, like an old mirror.

Signor Poerio has a warm smile and glasses with thick lenses that make his eyes small and distant. He seems protected by an indestructible candour; it must be his age, his sense of already

44

being a part of the past. The glass door opens on a largish room decorated in an old pink colour with narrow windows and a pattern of vine leaves painted along the ceiling moulding. The furniture is basic to the room's function: a nineteenth-century sofa, a stool with a Viennese wicker seat, a tailor's workbench in one corner. And then there are the manikins, a few busts upright on poles left standing here and there about the room in no particular order. And for a moment Spino imagines that they are Poerio's old customers, presences from the past who've transformed themselves into wooden manikins for old time's sake. Amongst them are some which do look like real people, with pink plaster faces that have turned almost brown and small white peelings on their cheekbones or noses. They are men with square jaws and short sideburns, plaster hair-styles imitating the Brylcreem look, thin lips and rather languid eyes. Poerio shows Spino some catalogues to help him choose a model. They must be catalogues from the sixties. The trousers are narrow and the jacket lapels long and pointed. He pauses a moment over one of the less ridiculous, more discreet models, then arranges the dead man's jacket on a manikin and has the tailor look at it. If he could make him one like this, what does he reckon? Poerio considers, he's puzzled, twists his mouth wrily. 'It's a sporty jacket,' he says doubtfully, 'I don't know if it would be right for the kind of suit you're after.' Spino agrees. Still, the old jacket has such a perfect cut that it wouldn't look out of place as a regular suit either. He shows the tailor the nametag inside, sewn onto the pocket. Poerio has no trouble recognising it. It's his tag, though straight off he can't remember anything about the jacket. It's an old jacket, he has put together so many jackets in his time . . .

Spino says he appreciates that, but with a bit of effort could he remember something, that is, find the invoice . . . an old accounts register maybe? Poerio thinks about it. He has taken a flap of the jacket between forefinger and thumb and strokes the fabric thoughtfully. One thing he is sure of, he made it in the sixties, absolutely no doubt about that, it was part of a small roll of cloth, he remembers it perfectly, a remnant that cost him next to nothing because it was a warehouse leftover and the supplier wanted to get rid of it. Poerio now seems a little suspicious, he's not sure what Spino wants of him. 'Are you from the police?' he asks. All of a sudden he's turned wary, obviously he's afraid of saying something that might harm him.

Spino tries to reassure him somehow: no, he says, he really does want a suit, there's nothing to worry about, on the contrary, he'd like to put down a deposit right away; and then he mumbles a strange explanation. It's pretty contrived and Poerio doesn't seem at all convinced. Still, he says he's willing to help, as far as he can. He does still have his little file of past customers, although many must be dead. To be honest he closed the

46

shop eight years back, he laid off his apprentices and retired. There was no reason for keeping the business going any more.

'Well then, let's see . . . let's see,' he whispers, leafing mechanically through blocks of receipts. 'This one is '59, but there are a few orders from 1960 as well . . .' He reads them carefully, holding the blocks a few inches from his nose. He's taken his glasses off and his eyes are childlike. 'This is it, I think,' he announces with a certain satisfaction. ' "Jacket in *real tweed.*" Yes, it must be this one.' He pauses a moment. ' "Guglielmo Faldini, Accountant, Tirrenica, Via della Dogana 15 (red)." ' He lifts his eyes from the receipt and puts his glasses back on. He says that actually now he's thought about it he doesn't feel up to making a suit. His eyesight's so bad he can't even thread a needle. And then he wouldn't be able to make the kind of suits people are wearing these days.

12

He finds Faldini, the accountant, in a dusty office where, on a glass door leading to a dark corridor, a frosted sign says: 'Tirrenica Import–Export'. The window offers a view of harbour derricks, a sheet-iron warehouse and a tugboat pitching in an oily sea. Faldini has the face of someone who has spent his entire life addressing letters to distant countries while looking out across a landscape of derricks and containers. Under a sheet of glass, his desk is a patchwork of postcards. Behind him a brightly-coloured calendar extols the delights of holidays in Greece. He has a placid look about him, big watery eyes, grey hair cut short and bristling in an old-fashioned style. He is truly amazed to see his jacket again. He lost it so many years ago. No, he couldn't say how many. Well, twenty maybe.

'You really lost it?'

Faldini toys with a pencil on his desk. The tug has moved through the frame of the window leaving light blue patches on the water. It's hard to say. He doesn't know. Or rather, he thinks not, let's say that it disappeared, so far as he can recall. From the harbour, in the distance, comes the

sound of a siren. The accountant considers his
visitor with a certain curiosity. Obviously he's
asking himself, what on earth's this business of
my old jacket, who is this man, what's he after?
And Spino finds it so difficult to be convincing,
and then he's not really trying. Faldini watches
him with his placid expression. Of course, on the
accounts book he keeps open in front of him there
are numbers that tell of dream cities like Samark-
and, where people maybe have a different way of
being people. Spino feels he must tell him the
truth, or something like the truth. So then, this
is the truth, this is how things stand. Does he
understand, this Faldini, the accountant? Perhaps. Or rather he senses it somehow, the same
way he must sense his sedentary man's dreams.
But it doesn't matter, yes, he remembers. It was in
'59, or maybe '60. He always hung the jacket
there, where he hangs the jacket he has now. On
that coathanger behind the door. The office was
exactly as it is now, identical. He makes a vague
gesture in the air. In his memory the only thing
different is himself, a young Faldini, a young
accountant, who would never go to Samarkand.
And there was a workman, a sort of porter, that
is. He often came into the office, did a bit of
everything. He did it because he needed the work,
but in the past, if Faldini remembers rightly, he'd
had a clerical position at the Customs. He doesn't
know why he'd lost that job. He'd had some
personal catastrophe, he doesn't know what. He
was a reserved, polite person, ill perhaps, he

49

wasn't cut out for being a porter. His name was Fortunato, sometimes names are really ironic, but everyone called him Cordoba. He can't remember his surname. They called him Cordoba because he'd been out in Argentina, or some other Latin American country, yes, his wife had died in Argentina and he had come back to Italy with his son, a little boy. He always talked about his little boy, on the rare occasions when he did talk. He had no relatives here and he'd put him in a boarding school. That is, it wasn't a proper boarding school, it was a lodging house run by an old maid who kept a few children, a sort of private school, but on a small scale, where it was he wouldn't know, he has a vague impression it was near Santo Stefano, the church, perhaps. The boy was called Carlito. Cordoba was always talking about Carlito.

A phone rings in a nearby room. Faldini is brought up short, coming back to the present. He casts a worried glance towards the door and then to his accounts books. The morning is flying by, say his eyes now, eyes in which Spino also catches an intimation of constraint and embarrassment. Well then, one last thing and he'll be off. If he'd just like to take a look at this photograph. This man sitting under the porch here, could it be Cordoba? Does he recognise him? And the boy? The accountant holds the photo delicately between thumb and forefinger. He holds it at arm's length, he's long-sighted. No, he says, it's not Cordoba, although, odd, it does look very like him, maybe it's his brother, though he doesn't know if Cordoba had a brother. As for the boy, he never saw Carlito.

Faldini is toying nervously with his pencil now. He seems distracted. Yes, well, he wouldn't like to have been misunderstood, you know, belongings, they're always so slippery, these belongings of ours, they move about, they even get the better of your memory. How could he not have remembered? In any case, now he remembers perfectly. He gave that jacket to Cordoba. He gave it to him as a present one day. Cordoba was always badly dressed, and he was a decent person.

13

'They say I'm mad because I live alone with all these cats, but what do I care? You haven't come about the gate, have you? The front gate. I had to have it repainted because a council van scraped it right across trying to turn round. It happened a while ago, you should know better than me, shouldn't you? Anyway, of course I remember Carlito. But I'm not sure if he's the boy in your photograph. You see, the boy in the photo looks too blond to be him, but then you never can tell. The Carlito I had here was a cheerful boy. He loved all the little creatures you find in the earth: beetles, ants, fireflies, green-and-yellow caterpillars, the ones with the sticking-out eyes and the furry bits . . .'

The cat curled up in her lap shakes itself and with a jump bounds away. She gets up too. She still has some photographs, she never throws anything away, she likes to keep things. From a drawer she takes out some little boxes, ribbons, rosary beads, a mother-of-pearl album. She invites him to look through the album with her. Two pairs of eyes are better than one. There are yellowing photographs of surly men leaning on fake cardboard parapets with the name of the photographer stamped under their feet; and then an infantryman with an unhappy expression, this with a dedication written at an angle; then a view of Vittorio Veneto in 1918, an old woman sitting on a wicker armchair, a view of Florence with carriages in the streets, a church, a family portrait taken from too far away, a girl with white gloves and hands pressed together, memento of a first communion. There are some empty pages, a dog with melancholy eyes, a house with wistaria and shutters under which a feminine hand has written: *scent of a summer*. On the last page a group of children have been arranged in pyramid shape in a little courtyard. The ones in front are crouching, then there's a row standing, and finally another higher row – perhaps the photographer had them climb on a bench. He counts them. There are twenty-four. On their right, standing and with her hands held together, is Signorina Elvira as she was then, although really she hasn't changed that much. The children have been arranged too far from the lens for their faces to be recognised with any confidence. The only one who might in some way resemble the face he is looking for is a little blond boy in the front row. His body has the same posture, chin propped up on one hand with the elbow resting on his knee. But definite identification is impossible.

And does Signorina Elvira remember the boy's father? No, not the father. All she knows is that he was dead, the mother too, all the boy had was

Switches from dialogue to
narrative often

an uncle. But is he sure he was called Carlito? She seems to remember Carlino. Anyhow, it's not important. He was a cheerful boy. He loved the little creatures you find in the earth: beetles, ants, fireflies, green-and-yellow caterpillars . . .

And so here he is again wandering about in search of nothing. The walls of these narrow streets seem to promise a reward he never manages to arrive at, as if they formed the board of a game of snakes and ladders, full of dead ends and trap-doors, on which he goes up and down, round and round, hoping that sooner or later the dice will take him to a square that will give the whole thing meaning. And meanwhile over there is the sea. He looks at it. Across its surface pass the shapes of ships, a few seagulls, clouds.

14

There are days when the jealous beauty of this city seems to unveil itself. On clear days, for example, windy days, when the breeze that announces the arrival of the south-westerly sweeps along the streets slapping like a taut sail. Then the houses and bell-towers take on a brightness that is too real, the outlines too sharp; like a photograph with fierce contrasts, light and shade collide aggressively without blending together, forming a black-and-white check of splashes of shadow and dazzling light, of alleyways and small squares.

Once, if he had nothing else to do, he used to choose days like this to wander round the old dock area, and now, following the dead-end sidings the wagons use along the quay, heading back to town, he finds himself thinking of those days. He could catch the bus that goes to town through the tunnels of the circular, but instead he chooses to walk across the docks, following the twists and turns of the wharves. He feels he wants to dawdle slowly through this grim landscape of railway lines that reminds him of his childhood, of diving from the landing stage with the tyres along its sides, of those poor summers, the memory of which has remained etched inside him like a scar.

In the disused shipyard, where once they used to repair steamships, he sees the hulk of a Swedish vessel lying on its side. It's called the *Ulla*. Strangely, the yellow letters of the name somehow escaped the fire that devastated the boat leaving enormous brown stains on the paint. And he has the impression that this old monster on the brink of extinction has always been there in that corner of the dock. A little further on he found a battered phonebox. He thought of phoning Corrado to put him in the picture. Anyway it was only right to let him know, since to a certain extent he owed the meeting to his friend.

'Corrado,' he said, 'it's me. I managed to speak to him.'

'But where are you? Why did you disappear like that?'

'I didn't disappear at all. I'm at the docks. Don't worry.'

'Sara was after you. She left you a message here at the paper. She says they're extending their holiday for three days, they're going to Switzerland.'

A seagull, which had been wheeling about for some time, landed on the arm of a waterpump right next to the phonebox and stood there quietly watching him while at the same time hunting through its feathers with its beak.

'There's a seagull next to me, it's right here next to the phonebox, it's as if it knew me.'

'What are you on about? . . . Listen, where did you find him, what did he tell you?'

'I can't explain now. There's a seagull here with its ears pricked, it must be a spy.'

'Don't play the fool. Where are you, where did you find him?'

'I told you, I'm at the docks. We met at the Boat Club. There are boats for hire and we went out for a trip.'

Corrado's voice dropped, perhaps someone had come into the office. 'Don't trust him,' he said. 'Don't trust him an inch.'

'It's not a question of trusting or not. He gave me a tip and I'm going to try it out. He didn't know anything about the business. But there's someone who maybe does know something and he told me who.'

'Who?'

'I told you I can't tell you, I don't want to speak on the phone.'

'There's no one here who can hear you. You can speak on my phone. Tell me who.'

'Come on, you don't imagine he went and gave me name and surname, do you? He's very smart. He just gave me an idea.'

'So then, give me an idea.'

'You wouldn't understand.'

'So how come you understood?'

'Because it's someone I happened to know years back. A musician.'

'Where does he play?'

'Corrado, please, I can't tell you anything.'

'In any event I don't like it, and you're too naive, understand? It's a quicksand. Anywhere you put your feet you risk sinking in.'

'Sorry, Corrado, have to say goodbye, it's getting late. And then this seagull is getting annoyed, he wants to make a call, he's waving his beak at me furiously.'

'Come straight here, I'll wait for you at the paper. I won't go home, specially so I can see you.'

'What about tomorrow, okay? I'm tired now, and I've got something to do this evening.'

'Promise me you won't trust anyone.'

'Okay, talk to you tomorrow.'

'Hang on a second, I heard something that might interest you. The coroner has arranged for the burial, the case has been dropped.'

15

Twenty years ago the Tropical was a small nightclub with a seedy atmosphere catering for American sailors. Now it's called the Lousiana and it's a piano bar with couches and table lamps. On the drinks list, on a green velvet noticeboard near the main door, it says: *Piano player – Peppe Harpo*.

Peppe Harpo is Giuseppe Antonio Arpetti, born in Sestri Levante in 1929, struck off the register of doctors in 1962 for his overlavish prescription of addictive drugs. In his university days he played the piano at little parties. He was quite talented and could do perfect imitations of Erroll Garner. After the drug scandal he took to playing at the Tropical. He played mamboes and pop songs through evenings thick with smoke, five hundred lire a drink. The emergency exit, behind the curtains, opened onto a stairwell where, above another door, a neon sign said: *Pensione – Zimmer – Rooms*. Then at a certain point he disappeared for six or seven years, to America, people said. When he reappeared it was with small round spectacles and a greying moustache. He had become Peppe Harpo, the jazz pianist. And with his return the Tropical became the Louisiana. Some said he had bought the place, that he'd made money playing in bands in America. That he had made money no one found strange. He seemed capable of it. That he had made money banging on the piano left many unconvinced.

Spino sat down at a table to one side and ordered a gin and tonic. Harpo was playing 'In a Little Spanish Town', and Spino supposed his entry had passed unobserved, but then when his drink came there was no bill with it. He sat on his own for a long time, slowly sipping his gin and listening to old tunes. Then towards eleven Harpo took a break and a tape of dance music took over from the piano. Spino had the impression, as Harpo came towards him through the tables, that his face wore an expression at once remorseful and resolute, as if he were thinking: ask me anything, but not that, I can't tell you that. *He knows*, a voice inside him whispered, *Harpo knows*. For a second Spino thought of putting the photo of the Kid as a child down on the table and then saying nothing, just smiling with the sly expression of one who knows what he knows. Instead he said straightforwardly that perhaps the time had come for Harpo to return him that favour. He was sorry if that was putting it bluntly. The favour, that is, of helping him find somebody, as he had once helped Harpo. A look of what seemed like genuine amazement crossed Harpo's face. He waited without saying anything. So Spino pulled out the group photograph. 'Him,' he said, pointing at the boy.

'Is he a relative of yours?'

Spino shook his head.

'Who is he?'

'I don't know. That's what I want to find out. Perhaps his name is Carlito.'

Harpo looked at Spino suspiciously, as if expecting a trick, or afraid he was being made fun of. Was he mad? The people were wearing fifties-style clothes, it was an old photograph. The boy must be a man now, for God's sake.

'You know perfectly well what I'm talking about,' Spino said. 'He's got a dark beard now. His hair is darker too, not as light as in the photo, but his face still has something boyish about it. He's been in my freezer for a few days. The people who knew him are keeping quiet, nothing, not even an anonymous phone call, as if he'd never existed. They're wiping out his past.'

Harpo was looking around rather uneasily. A couple at a nearby table was watching them with interest. 'Don't speak so loud,' he said. 'No need to disturb the customers.'

'Listen, Harpo,' Spino said, 'if a person doesn't have the courage to go beyond appearances, he'll never understand, will he? All his life he'll just be forced to keep playing the game without understanding why.'

Harpo called a waiter and ordered a drink. 'But who's he to you?' he asked softly. 'You don't know him, he doesn't mean anything to you.' He was speaking in a whisper, uneasy, his hands moving nervously.

'And you?' Spino said. 'Who are you to yourself? Do you realise that if you wanted to find that out one day you'd have to look for yourself all over the place, reconstruct yourself, rummage in old drawers, get hold of evidence from other people, clues scattered here and there and lost? You'd be completely in the dark, you'd have to feel your way.'

Harpo lowered his voice even further and told him to try an address, though he wasn't certain. His face told Spino that in giving him that address the favour had been repaid in full.

16

It's called 'Egle's'. It's an old pie-house, or that's what he's heard people call it. The walls are covered in white tiles and behind a zinc-topped counter Signora Egle bustles about a small wood-fired oven serving cakes and pies. Spino sits at one of the little marble tables and a grey-aproned waitress with the haggard look of a cloistered nun comes with a cloth to wipe up the crumbs the last customer left. He orders a chickpea pie and then, as instructed, lays a copy of the *Gazzetta Ufficiale* on the table in full view. He begins to check out the other customers and speculate as to who they are. At the table next to his are two middle-aged blonde women chattering in low voices, occasionally exploding in shrill laughter. They look well-heeled and are wearing vulgar, expensive clothes. They could be two retired whores who've invested their earnings well and now run a shop, or some business related to their previous profession, but dignified now by this façade of respectability. Sitting in a corner is a young lout bundled up in a thick jacket and engrossed in a magazine from the cover of which a fat orange-clad guru wags a warning

63

finger at the plate of pie in front of him. Then there's a spry-looking old man, hair dyed a black that takes on a reddish tint about the temples, as cheap dyes often do. He has a gaudy tie and brown-and-white shoes with patterns of tiny holes. Wheeler-dealer, pimp, widower in the grip of a mad desire for adventure? Could be anything. Finally there's a lanky man leaning against the counter. He's chatting to Signora Egle and smiling, showing off an enormous gap in his upper teeth. He has a horsey profile and greased-back hair, a jacket that doesn't manage to cover his bony wrists, jeans. Signora Egle seems determined not to concede something the lanky character is insisting on. Then, with an expression of surrender, she moves to one end of the counter and puts a record on a decrepit gramophone that had looked as if it were purely decorative. The record is a 78 and rumbles; there are a couple of bursts from a band and then a falsetto voice starts up, distorted by the scratches the disc carries in its grooves. Incredibly, it's '*Il tango delle capinere*', sung by Rabagliati. The lanky character sends a nod of complicity in the direction of the waitress and she, unresisting but sullen, lets herself be led in a long-stepping tango that immediately captures the attention of the clientele. The girl leans a cheek on the chest of her beau, which is as far as her height allows her to reach, but she's having all kinds of trouble keeping up with his powerful strides as he leads her aggressively about the room. They finish

with a supple *casqué* and everybody claps. Even
Spino joins in, then opens his paper, pushing his
plate away, and pretends to be absorbed in the
Gazzetta Ufficiale.

Meanwhile the boy with the guru on his
magazine gets up dreamily and pays his bill.
Going out he doesn't deign anyone in the room a
single glance, as if he had too much on his mind.
The two big blonde women are repairing their
make-up and two cigarettes with traces of lipstick
on the filters burn in their ashtray. They leave
chuckling, but no one shows any special interest
in Spino, nor in the paper he's reading. He raises
his eyes from the paper and his gaze meets that
of the spry old man. There follows a long and
intense exchange of glances and Spino feels a light
coating of sweat on the palms of his hands. He
folds his paper and puts his pack of cigarettes on
top, waiting for the first move. Perhaps he should
do something, he thinks, but he's not sure what.
Meanwhile the girl has finished clearing the
tables and has started spreading damp sawdust
on the floor, sweeping it along the tiles with a
broom taller than herself. Signora Egle is going
through the day's takings behind the counter.
The room is quiet now, the air thick with breath,
with cigarettes, with burnt wood. Then the spry
little old man smiles: it's a trite, mechanical smile,
accompanied by the slightest jerk of the head and
then another gesture that tells all. Spino sees
the misunderstanding he's been encouraging,
immediately turns red with embarrassment, then

65

senses, rising within him, a blind anger and intolerance towards this place, towards his own stupidity. He makes a sign to the girl and asks for his bill. She approaches wearily, drying her hands on her apron. She tots up his bill on a paper napkin; her hands are red and swollen with a coating of sawdust sticking to their backs, they might be two chops sprinkled with breadcrumbs. Then, giving him an insolent look, she mutters in a toneless voice: 'You're losing your hair. Reading after eating makes you lose your hair.' Spino looks at her astonished, as though not believing his ears. It can't be her, he thinks, it can't be. And he almost has to hold himself back from attacking this little monster who goes on giving him her arrogant stare. But she, still in that detached, professional tone, is telling him about a herbalist who sells things for hair, on Vico Spazzavento.

17

Vico Spazzavento – Windswept Lane – is the perfect name for this blind alley squeezed between walls covered with scars. The wind forms a whirling eddy right where a blade of sunshine, slipping into the narrow street between flapping washing seen high above against a corridor of sky, lights up a little heap of swirling detritus. A wreath of dry flowers, newspapers, a nylon stocking.

The shop is in a basement with a swing door. It looks like a coal cellar, and in fact on the floor there are some sacks of coal, although the sign on the doorpost says: 'spices, paints'. On the counter is a pile of newspapers used to wrap up goods sold. A little old man dozing on a small wicker-covered chair near the coal got to his feet. Spino was first to say hello. The old man mumbled a good evening. He propped himself up against the counter with a lazy and seemingly absent expression.

'Someone told me you sold hair lotions here,' Spino said.

The old man answered knowledgeably. He leant over the counter a little to look at Spino's hair, listed various products with curious names: *Zolfex*, *Catramina*. Then some plants and roots: sage, nettle, rhubarb, red cedar. He thinks red cedar is what he needs, that's his guess at first glance, though one ought to do some tests on the hair.

Spino answered that maybe red cedar would be okay, he doesn't know, he doesn't know what properties red cedar has.

The old man looked at him doubtfully. He had metal-framed spectacles and a two-day growth of beard. He didn't say anything. Spino tried not to let his nerves get the better of him. Calmly, he explained that he hadn't checked out his hair type, it was just brittle. In any case, he doesn't want a commercial product, he wants a special lotion. He stressed the word special, something that *only* the shopkeeper knows the formula for. He has come on the advice of people he trusts. It's strange they haven't mentioned it to him.

The old man pushed aside a curtain, said to wait and disappeared. For a second Spino caught a glimpse of a poky little room with a gas-ring and a lightbulb switched on, but he didn't see anybody. The old man started to speak, a few yards from Spino, in a whisper. A woman's voice answered, perhaps an old woman. Then they fell silent. Then they began to speak again, their voices very low. It was impossible to catch what they were saying. Then came a squeak as of a drawer being opened, and finally silence again.

The minutes passed slowly. Not a sound came

from beyond the curtain now, as if the two had gone out by another door leaving him waiting there like an idiot. Spino coughed loudly, he made a noise with a chair, at which the old man reappeared at the curtain with a look of reproach. 'Be patient,' he said, 'another few minutes.'

He came out round the counter and went to close and bolt the swing door that opened onto the street. He moved somewhat cautiously, looked at his customer, lit a small cigar, and returned to the back room. The voices began to whisper again, more urgently than before. The shop was almost dark. The daylight coming in through the small barred window had grown dimmer. The sacks of coal along the walls looked like human bodies abandoned in sleep. Spino couldn't help thinking that the dead man might also have come to this shop once and like him have waited in the half-dark; perhaps the old man knew him well, knew who he was, his reasons, his motives.

Finally the little man came back, all smiles. In his hand he had a small brown bottle of the kind they use in pharmacies to sell iodine. He wrapped it up carefully in a sheet of newspaper and pushed it across the counter without a word. Spino looked at it now, paused, smiled perhaps. 'Hope you're not making a mistake,' he said. 'It's important.'

The old man released the bolt on the door, went back to sit on his seat and started on the accounts he had previously broken off. He made a show of pretending not to have heard. 'Off you go now,' he said. 'The instructions are on the label.'

Spino slipped the little bottle into his pocket and left. When he said goodbye, the old man answered that he had put some sage in the lotion too, to give it some fragrance. And Spino had the impression he was still smiling. There was no one in Vico Spazzavento. He felt as though time hadn't passed, as though everything had happened too quickly, like some event that took place long ago and is revisited in the memory in a flash.

18

He asked the caretaker if he knew of a monument with an angel and an owl. The caretaker looked at the visitor and pretended to concentrate, though it was perfectly obvious he was disorientated. All the same, so as not to seem ignorant of course, he said it must be in the Western Gallery, and in revenge flaunted a knowledge that hadn't been asked for. 'It must be one of the first graves,' he said. 'During the Romantic period the owl was in fashion.' Then, as Spino was walking away in the direction indicated by his outstretched arm, the caretaker reminded him that the cemetery closed at five and that he'd better be careful not to get locked inside. 'There's always someone gets left in, you know,' he added, as if to tone down the bluntness of his warning.

Spino nodded to show he had understood and set off along the asphalt avenue that cuts across the central squares. The cemetery was all but deserted, perhaps because it was late and the weather was unpleasantly windy. A few little old women dressed in black were busy in the squares tidying the graves. It's strange how one can spend one's life in a city without getting to know one of its most famous sites. Spino had never set foot in this cemetery described in all the tourist guides. He thought that to get to know a cemetery maybe you had to have your own dead there, and his dead were not in this place, nor in any other, and now that he was at last visiting the cemetery it was because he had acquired one of the dead who was not his own and was not buried here and to whom he was not even connected by any memories of a common past.

He began to wander about among the graves, distractedly reading the stones of the recently dead. Then his curiosity drew him towards the steps of the ugly neoclassical temple which houses the urns of some of the great men of the Risorgimento and along the pediment of which a Latin inscription establishes an incongruous connection between God and country. He crossed a section of the eastern part of the cemetery where bizarrely ornamented graves, all spires and pinnacles, loom alongside ugly little neo-gothic palaces. And he could hardly help but notice how at a certain period all the titled dead of the city had been concentrated in this area: nobles, senators of the realm, admirals, bishops; and then families for whom the nobility of wealth had stood in for the rarer nobility of blood: shipbuilders, merchants, the first industrialists. From the pronaos of the temple one can make out the original geometry of the cemetery which later developments were to change considerably. But the concept it expressed has remained unchanged: to the south and east, the aristocracy; to the north and west, the monumental tombs of the bourgeois business class; in the central squares, in the ground, the common people. Then there are a few areas for floating categories, for those who don't belong; he noticed a portico beside the steps of the temple entirely given over to philanthropists: benefactors, men of science, intellectuals of various levels. It's curious how nineteenth-century Italy faithfully reproduced in its choreography of death the class divisions that operated in life. He lit a cigarette and sat down at the top of the steps, immersed in his thoughts. *Battleship Potemkin* came to mind, as it does every time he sees an enormous, white flight of steps. And then a film about the Fascist period that he had liked for its sets. For a moment he had the impression that he too was in a scene in a film and that a director, from a low angle, behind an invisible movie camera, was filming him sitting there thinking. He looked at his watch and reassured himself it was only a quarter past four. So then, he still had fifteen minutes before the appointment. He set off along the Western Gallery, stopping to look at the monuments and read the inscriptions. He stood a long time in front of the statue of the hazelnut seller, studying her carefully. Her face was modelled with a realism that showed no mercy in reproducing the features of a plebeian physiognomy. It was obvious that the old woman had posed for the sculpture in her Sunday best: the lace bodice peeps out from under a working

73

woman's shawl, a smart skirt covers the heavy pleats of another skirt, her feet are in slippers. With the hazelnuts she sold her whole life at street corners strung in loops over her arms, she stands to have the statue sculpted, this statue that now, life-size, looks out at the visitor with pride. A little further on an inscription on a bas-relief clumsily representing the throne of the Ludovisi informs him that Matilde Giappichelli Roma-nengo, a virtuous and kindly woman, having scarcely passed her thirtieth year, left husband and daughters Lucrezia and Federiga distraught. The deceased passed away on the second day of September 1886, and the two daughters, who dutifully hold the sheet from which their mother Matilde is flying to heaven, also support an inscription alongside which says: 'Dear Mummy, what shall we offer you if not prayers and flowers?'

He walked slowly along the gallery until he found the grave with the angel and the owl. He noticed that a solitary seagull, blown along perhaps by the south-west wind, was hovering over the squares as if intending to land. On days like this when the south-westerly blows hard it's not unusual to see seagulls even in those parts of the city furthest from the coast. They flock in, following the rubbish-strewn canal, then wander away from the water looking for food. It was exactly half past four. Spino sat on the low wall of the gallery, his back to the tomb, and lit another cigarette. There was no one under the porticos along the gallery and the old women in the middle of the squares had thinned out. Over to the other side of the squares, in a corner near the cypresses, he noticed a man who seemed deep in contemplation near a cross, and started to watch him. The minutes passed slowly but the man made no move. Then he got up quickly and set off towards the small square by the exit. Spino looked around, but could see no one. His watch indicated that it was a quarter to five, and he realised that no one would be coming now to keep this strange appointment. Or perhaps no one was supposed to come, they had simply wanted to know if he would, and now someone he couldn't see was watching him perhaps, was checking that he really was willing. It was a kind of test they had set him.

The seagull touched down lightly just a few yards away and began to walk awkwardly between the graves, quietly curious, like a pet. Spino felt in his pocket and threw it a sweet which the bird immediately swallowed, shaking its head from side to side and fluffing out its feathers in satisfaction. Then it took off for a moment, not much more than a jump, to come to rest on the shoulder of a little First World War soldier, from where it looked at him calmly. 'Who are you?' Spino asked him softly. 'Who sent you? You were spying on me at the docks too. What do you want?'

It was two minutes to five. Spino got up quickly and his brusque movement frightened the seagull, which took off obliquely to glide away over the other square near the steps. Before leaving, Spino glanced at the tomb with the angel and the owl and read the inscription which, in the suspense of waiting, he had overlooked. Only then did it come to him that someone had merely wanted him to read that inscription, this was what the appointment amounted to, this was the message. Under a foreign name, on a bas-relief scroll, was a Greek motto, and beside it the translation: Man's body dies; virtue does not die.

He began to run and the noise of his footsteps echoed high up under the vaults of the gallery. When he reached the exit the caretaker was sliding the gate along its rail and Spino bid him a hurried goodnight: 'There's a seagull still inside,' he said. 'I think he's planning to sleep there.' The man said nothing in reply. He took off his peaked cap and pushed back the hair on an almost bald scalp.

19

He found the message in his letterbox on returning home: a note written in capital letters indicating a time and place.

He put it in his pocket and climbed the stairs of his old block. As he entered his flat the bell-tower of San Donato began to strike six. He ran to the door leading out to the terrace and threw it open, wanting the sound to come right into the flat and fill it. He took off his tie and flopped down on an armchair, putting his feet up on the coffee table. From this position all he could see was the outline of the bell-tower, the slate of a roof and then a stretch of the horizon. He found a white sheet of paper and wrote in large capitals like those in the message: 'Weep? What's Hecuba to him?'

He placed the paper next to the note and thought of the connection between them. He was tempted to phone Corrado and tell him: 'Corrado, you remember this line? I've understood exactly what it means.' He looked at the phone but didn't move. He realised that he wouldn't be able to explain. Perhaps he would put it in a letter to Sara, but without offering long explanations, just write it as now he had intuitively understood

it, and as she too would understand, that the
player who was weeping (but who was he?) saw,
albeit in another shape and in another fashion,
himself in Hecuba. He thought of the power
things have to come back to us and of how much
of ourselves we see in others. And like a wave
sweeping across him, warm and overwhelming,
he remembered a deathbed and a promise made
and never kept. And now that promise demanded
fulfilment, it was obvious, found in him and in
this quest a kind of accomplishment, a different
kind, an apparently incongruous kind, but one
which in fact followed an implacable logic, as of
some unknown geometry, something one might
intuit but could never pin down in a rational
order or in an explanation. And he thought that
things do follow an order and that nothing
happens by chance, that chance in fact is just this:
our incapacity to grasp the true connections
between things. And he sensed the vulgarity and
the arrogance with which we bring together the
objects that surround us. He looked about him
and thought, what was the connection between
the jug on the chest of drawers and the window?
They weren't related in any way, they were
foreign to each other; they seemed plausible to
him only because one day, many years ago, he
had bought that jug and put it on the chest of
drawers near the window. The only connection
between the two objects was his eyes looking at
them. Yet something, something more than this
must have led his hand to buy that jug. And that

forgotten, hurried gesture was the real connection; everything lay in that gesture, the world and life, and a universe.

And once again he thought of that young man, and now he saw the scene clearly. It had happened like this, he knew it. He saw him come out of his hiding-place and deliberately put himself in the path of the bullets, seeking out the exact position that would bring him his death. He saw him advance down the corridor with calculated determination, as if following the geometry of a particular trajectory so as to accomplish an expiation or achieve a simple connection between events. That was what Carlo Nobodi had done, who as a child had been called Carlito. He had established a connection. Through him things apparently unconnected had found a way of tracing their pattern.

So he took the paper where he'd written the question about Hecuba and pegged it out on the washing line on the terrace, then came back in, sat in the same position as before, and looked at it. The paper fluttered like a flag in the stiff breeze. It was a bright, rustling stain against the falling night. He just watched it for a long time, establishing again a connection between that piece of paper flapping in the dusk and the line of the horizon that was ever so slowly dissolving away into darkness. The vanishing point. He got up slowly, overcome by a great tiredness. But it was a calm, peaceful tiredness that led him by the hand towards his bed as if he were a boy again.

79

And that night he had a dream. It was a dream he hadn't had for years, too many years. It was a childish dream and he felt light and innocent; and dreaming, he had the curious awareness of having rediscovered this dream, and this heightened his innocence, like a liberation.

20

He spent the day putting his books in order. It's incredible how many newspapers and notes can accumulate in a house. He threw away whole stacks of them, cleaning up the couch and the corners where they had piled up over the years. Likewise out in the rubbish went all sorts of things from the bottoms of drawers, old stuff, the kind of bric-à-brac you can never see your way to throwing out, either from laziness or because of that indefinable sadness that objects connected with our past arouse. When he'd finished, it was as if it were another flat. How pleased Sara would be, poor thing, having put up with that indescribable mess for so long. In the evening he wrote her a letter and sealed it in an envelope he had already stamped, intending to post it on his way to the appointment. Then he telephoned Corrado, but only got the answering machine. He had to hang up because straight off he found himself unable to leave the message the recorded voice was asking for. Then he prepared something and dialled again. 'Hi, Corrado,' he said, 'Spino here, I just wanted to say hello and tell you that I think of you with affection.'

flashback (?)

Hanging up, he was reminded of a day many years before when he had dialled the same number and said: 'Corrado, it's me again, you remember that day we went to see *Picnic* and fell in love with Kim Novak?' Only when he had put the receiver down did he realise that he'd said something ridiculous, but by then it was too late to do anything about it. Then he thought that maybe Corrado wouldn't find it ridiculous, perhaps it would just seem strange hearing it on the answering machine.

At dinnertime he made himself a snack with a tin of salmon he'd had in the fridge heaven knows how long and some pineapple doused in port. When evening fell he turned on the radio without putting on the light and sat in the dark smoking and looking out of the window at the lights in the harbour. He let the time slip by. He enjoyed listening to the radio in the dark, it always gave him a sense of distance. Then the bell-tower of San Donato struck eleven and he started. He washed the dishes and tidied the kitchen in candlelight because he couldn't face the violence of the electric light. He left at half past eleven, locking the door and leaving the key under the flowerpot on the landing, where he always left it for Sara.

He posted the letter in the box near the newsagent's stand, took Vico dei Calafati and went down the steps as far as the road along the sea front. The trattorias by the harbour were closing; a little old man sunk up to his thighs in rubber boots was washing his fishmonger's counter with a hose. He went down the Ripa Gallery as far as the harbour railway station, then crossed the road and walked on along the tram-lines that have outlasted the asphalt there, keep-ing close to the safety fence between the two lines. A nightwatchman was heading in his direction on a moped and, passing by, wished him goodnight. He waited till he was some distance away, then slipped into the port area through a little turnstile next to the big gates of the Customs. There were still some lights on in the Customs building. He chose to cut across a small labyrinth of containers so as not to risk being seen. He walked along a wharf where a Revenue Department launch was tied up and found himself at the cargo docks. He went past the Old Wharf, cluttered with cotton bales, and stopped by the dry-docks. There was no trace of any human presence ahead of him now; the lights were all behind, the lamps of a ship moored to a wharf and two windows lit up in the harbour station. He walked on about five hundred metres, keeping the traffic-light hanging over the coast road to his right as a point of reference. Striking a match, he checked once again the route he was supposed to take, then screwed up the piece of paper and threw it in the water. He saw the dark outline of the warehouse under a skeleton of metal bridges. He sat down on an iron stairway at the water's edge and lit a cigarette. The bell-tower of San Donato struck midnight. He hung on a few minutes more, looking out at the dark sea and an uncertain light on the horizon. To reach the warehouse he had to circle round some enormous containers scattered quite randomly along the wharf. The yard was lit by yellow foglights which drew four shadows from his body, projected in diametrically opposite directions, as if they wanted to flee from him at every step. He reached the back of the warehouse, going down the side where the dusty light of the lamps was weakest. On the handle of the door was a chain without a padlock and he slipped it out through the rings holding it. He eased open the door and a long strip of yellow light slid into the darkness inside, snapping at a right angle where it met a pile of crates. He coughed three times, keeping the coughs distinct and decisive, as he was supposed to, but there was no reply from inside the building. He stood immobile on the strip of light, coughed again, and again no one answered.

'It's me,' he said softly, 'I've come.'

He waited a moment, then repeated in a louder voice: 'It's me, I've come.' Only then did he suddenly feel absolutely certain that there was no one there. Despite himself he began to laugh, first softly, then more loudly. He turned round and looked at the water a few metres away. Then stepped forward into the dark.

The Woman of Porto Pim

The Woman of Porto Pim

Prologue

I am very fond of honest travel books and have always read plenty of them. They have the virtue of bringing an *elsewhere*, at once theoretical and plausible, to our inescapable, unyielding *here*. Yet an elementary sense of loyalty obliges me to put any reader who imagines that this little book contains a travel diary on his or her guard. The travel diary requires either a flair for on-the-spot writing or a memory untainted by the imagination that memory itself generates — qualities which, out of a paradoxical sense of realism, I have given up any hope of acquiring. Having reached an age at which it seems more dignified to cultivate illusions than foolish aspirations, I have resigned myself to the destiny of writing after my own fashion.

Having said this, it would nevertheless be dishonest to pass these pages off as pure fiction: the friendly, I might almost say pocket-size muse that dictated them, could not even remotely be compared with the majestic muse of Raymond Roussel, who managed to write his *Impressions d'Afrique* without ever stepping off his yacht. I did step off and put my feet on the ground, so that as well as being the product of my readiness to tell untruths this little book partly has its origins in the time I spent in the Azores. Basically, its subject matter is the whale, an animal which more than any other would seem to be a metaphor; and shipwrecks, which insofar as they are understood as failures and inconclusive adventures, would likewise appear to be metaphorical. My respect for the imaginations which conjured up Jonah and Captain Ahab has luckily saved me from any attempt to sneak myself, via literature, in amongst the ghosts and myths that inhabit our imaginations. If I talk about whales and shipwrecks, it is merely because in the Azores such phenomena can boast an unequivocal reality.

There are however two stories in this small volume which it would not be entirely inappropriate to define as fiction. The first, in its basic outline, is the life of Antero de Quental, great and unhappy poet who measured the depths of the universe and the human spirit within the brief compass of the sonnet. I owe to Octavio Paz's suggestion that poets have no biography and that their work is their biography, the idea of writing this story as if its subject were a fictional character. And then lives lost by the wayside, like Antero's, perhaps hold up better than others to being told along the lines of the hypothetical. The story which closes the book, on the other hand, I owe to the confidences of a man whom I may be supposed to have met in a tavern in Porto Pim. I won't rule out my having altered it with the kind of additions and motives typical of the presumption of one who believes that he can draw out the sense of a life just by telling its story. Perhaps it will be considered an extenuating circumstance if I confess that alcoholic beverages were consumed in abundance in this tavern and that I felt it would be impolite of me not to participate in the locally recognised custom.

The fragment of a story entitled 'Small Blue Whales Strolling about the Azores' can be thought of as a guided fiction, in the sense that it was prompted by a snatch of conversation overheard by chance. I don't even know myself what happened before and what afterwards. I presume it is about a kind of shipwreck: which is why I put it in the chapter where it is.

The piece entitled 'A Dream in Letter Form' I owe partly to reading Plato and partly to the rolling motion of a slow bus from Horta to Almoxarife. It may be that in the transition from dream to text the content has suffered some distortions, but each of us has the right to treat his dreams as he thinks fit. On the other hand the pages entitled 'A Hunt' aspire to no more than a factual account, the only merit they can claim being their trustworthiness. Similarly many other pages, and I feel it would be superfluous to say which, are mere transcripts of the real or of what others have written before me. Finally, the piece entitled 'A Whale's View of Man', in addition to my old vice of looking at things from another's point of view, unashamedly takes its inspiration from a poem by Carlos Drummond de Andrade, who, before myself, and better than myself, chose to see mankind through the sorrowful eyes of a slow animal. And it is to Drummond that this piece is humbly dedicated, partly in memory of an afternoon in Plinio Doyle's house in Ipanema when he told me about his childhood and about Halley's comet.

Vecchiano, 23 September 1982

Hesperides
A Dream in Letter Form

Having sailed for many days and many nights, I realised that the West has no end, but moves along with us, we can follow it as long as we like without ever reaching it. Such is the unknown sea beyond the Pillars, endless and always the same, and it is from that sea, like the thin backbone of an extinct colossus, that these small island crests rise up, knots of rock lost in the blue.

Seen from the sea, the first island you come to is a green expanse amidst which fruit gleams like gems, though sometimes what you may be seeing are strange birds with purple plumage. The coastline is impervious, black rock-faces inhabited by marauding sea birds which wail as twilight falls, flapping restlessly with an air of sinister torment. Rains are heavy and the sun pitiless: and because of this climate together with the island's rich black soil, the trees are extremely tall, the woods luxuriant and flowers abound, great blue and pink flowers, fleshy as fruit, such as I have never seen anywhere else. The other islands are rockier, though always rich in flowers and fruit, and the inhabitants get much of their food from the woods, and then the rest from the sea, since the water is warm and teeming with fish.

The men have light complexions and astonished eyes, as if the wonder at a sight once seen but now forgotten still played across their faces. They are silent and solitary, but not sad, and they will frequently laugh over nothing, like children. The women are handsome and proud, with prominent cheekbones and high foreheads. They walk with waterjugs on their heads and descending the steep flights of steps that lead to the water their bodies don't sway at all, so that they look like statues on which some god has bestowed the gift of movement. These people have no king, they know nothing of class or caste. There are no warriors because they have no need to wage war, having no neighbours. They do have priests, though of a special kind which I will tell you about later on. And anybody can become one, even the humblest peasant or beggar. Their Pantheon is not made up of gods like ours who preside over the sky, the earth, the sea, the underworld, the woods, the harvest, war and peace and the affairs of mankind. Instead they are gods of the spirit, of sentiments and passions. The principal deities are nine in number, like the islands in the archipelago, and each has his temple on a different island.

The god of Regret and Nostalgia is a child with an old man's face. His temple stands on the remotest of the islands in a valley protected by impenetrable mountains, near a lake, in a desolate, wild stretch of country. The valley is forever covered by a light mist, like a veil; there are tall beech trees which whisper in the breeze; a place of intense melancholy. To reach the temple you have to follow a path cut into the rock like the bed of a dried stream. And as you walk you come across strange skeletons of enormous unknown animals, fish perhaps, or maybe birds; and seashells, and stones the pink of mother-of-pearl. I called it a temple, but I ought to have said a shack: for the god of Regret and Nostalgia could hardly live in a palace or luxurious villa; instead he has but a hovel, poor as wept tears, something that stands amidst the things of this world with that same sense of shame as some secret sorrow lurking in our hearts. For this god is not only the god of Regret and Nostalgia; his deity extends to an area of the mind that includes remorse, and the sorrow for that which once was and which no longer causes sorrow but only the memory of sorrow, and the sorrow for that which never was but should have been, which is the most consuming sorrow of all. Men go to visit him dressed in wretched sackcloth, women cover themselves with dark cloaks; and they all stand in silence and sometimes you hear weeping, in the night, as the moon casts its silver light over the valley and over the pilgrims stretched out on the grass nursing their lifetime's regrets.

The god of Hatred is a little yellow dog with an emaciated look, and his temple stands on a tiny cone-shaped island: it takes many days and nights of travelling to get there and only real hatred, the hatred that swells the heart unbearably, spawned on envy and jealousy, could prompt the unhappy sufferer to undertake such an arduous voyage. Then there are the gods of Madness and of Pity, the god of Generosity and the god of Selfishness: but I never went to visit these gods and have heard only vague and fanciful stories in their regard.

As for their most important god, who would seem to be father of all the other gods and likewise of the earth and sky, the accounts I heard of him varied greatly, and I wasn't able to see his temple nor to approach his island. Not because foreigners are not allowed there, but because even the citizens of this republic can only go there after attaining a spiritual state which is but rarely achieved – and once there they do not come back. On this god's island stands a temple for which the inhabitants of the archipelago have a name I could perhaps translate as 'The Marvellous Dwellings'. It consists of a city which is entirely suppositional – in the sense that the buildings themselves don't exist; only their plans have been traced out on the ground. This city has the shape of a circular chessboard and stretches away for miles and miles: and every day, using simple pieces of chalk, the pilgrims move the buildings where they choose, as if they were chess pieces; so that the city is mobile and mutable, and its physiognomy is constantly changing. From the

94

centre of the chessboard rises a tower on the top of which rests an enormous golden sphere which vaguely recalls the fruit so abundant in the gardens of these islands. And this sphere is the god. I haven't been able to find out who exactly this god might be: the definitions offered me to date have been imprecise and tentative, not easily comprehensible to the foreigner perhaps. I presume that he has something to do with the idea of completeness, of plenitude, of perfection: a highly abstract idea, not easily comprehensible to the human intellect. Which is why I did think this might be the god of Happiness: but the happiness of those who have understood the sense of life so fully that death no longer has any importance for them; and that is why the chosen few who go to honour the god never return. The task of watching over this god has been given to an idiot with a doltish face and garbled speech who is perhaps in touch with the divinity in mysterious ways unknown to reason. When I expressed my desire to pay this god homage, people smiled at me and with an air of profound affection, which perhaps contained a hint of compassion, kissed me on both cheeks.

But I did pay homage along with others to the god of Love, whose temple stands on an island with white curving beaches on the bright sand washed by the sea. And the image of this god isn't an idol, nor anything visible, but a sound, the pure sound of sea water drawn into the temple through a channel carved from the rock and then breaking in a secret pool: and because of the shape of the walls and the size of the building, the sound from the pool reproduces itself in an endless echo, ravishing whoever hears it and inducing a sort of intoxication, or daze. And those who worship this god expose themselves to many and strange effects, since his is the principle which commands life, but it is a bizarre and capricious principle; and while it may be true that he is the soul and harmony of the elements, he can also produce illusions, ravings, visions. And on this island I witnessed spectacles that disturbed me in their innocent truth: so much so that I began to doubt whether such things really existed or whether they weren't rather the ghosts of my own feelings leaving my body to take shape and apparent reality in the air as a result of my exposing myself to the bewitching sound of the god. It was with such thoughts in my mind that I set out along a path that leads to the highest point of the island, whence you can see the sea on every side. At which I became aware that the island was deserted, that there was no temple on the beach and that the figures and faces of love I had seen like *tableaux vivants* and which included numerous gradations of the spirit, such as friendship, tenderness, gratitude, pride and vanity – all these aspects of love I thought I had seen in human form, were just mirages prompted by I don't know what enchantment. And thus I arrived right at the top of the promontory and as, observing the endless sea, I was already abandoning myself to the dejection that comes with disillusion, a blue cloud descended on me and carried me off in a dream: and I dreamed that I was writing you this letter, and that I was not the Greek who set sail to find the West and never came back, but was only dreaming of him.

I

Shipwrecks, Flotsam, Crossings, Distances

Small Blue Whales
Strolling about the Azores
Fragment of a Story

She owes me everything, said the man heat-edly, everything: her money, her success. I did it for her, I shaped her with my own hands, that's what. And as he spoke he looked at his hands, clenching and unclenching his fingers in a strange gesture, as if trying to grasp a shadow.

The small ferry began to change direction and a gust of wind ruffled the woman's hair. Don't talk like that, Marcel, please, she muttered, looking at her shoes. Keep your voice down, people are watching us. She was blonde and wore big sunglasses with delicately tinted lenses. The man's head jerked a little to one side, a sign of annoyance. Who cares, they don't understand, he answered. He tossed the stub of his cigarette into the sea and touched the tip of his nose as if to squash an insect. Lady Macbeth, he said with irony, the great tragic actress. You know the name of the place I found her in? It was called 'La Baguette', and as it happens she wasn't playing Lady Macbeth, you know what she was doing? The woman took off her glasses and wiped them nervously on her T-shirt. Please, Marcel, she said.

She was showing off her arse to a bunch of dirty old men, that's what our great tragic actress was doing. Once again he squashed the invisible insect on the tip of his nose. And I still have photographs, he said.

The sailor going round checking the tickets stopped in front of them and the woman rummaged in her bag. Ask him how much longer it'll be, said the man, I feel ill, this old bathtub is turning my stomach. The woman did her best to formulate the question in that strange language, and the sailor answered with a smile. About an hour and a half, she translated. The boat stops for two hours and then goes back. She put her glasses on again and adjusted her headscarf. Things aren't always what they seem, she said. What things? he asked. She smiled vaguely. Things, she said. And then went on: I was thinking of Albertine. The man grimaced, apparently impatient. You know what our great tragedian was called when she was at the Baguette? She was called Carole, Carole Don-Don. Nice, eh? He turned towards the sea, a wounded expression on his face, then came out with a small shout: Look! He pointed southwards. The woman turned and looked with him. On the horizon you could see the green cone of the island rising in sharp outline from the water. We're getting near, the man said, pleased now, I don't think it'll take an hour and a half. Then he narrowed his eyes and leaned on the railings. There are rocks too, he added. He moved his arm to the left and pointed to two deep-blue outcrops, like two hats laid on the water. What nasty rocks, he said, they look like cushions. I can't see them, said the woman. There, said Marcel, a little bit more to the left, right in line with my finger, see? He slipped his right arm around the woman's shoulder, keeping his hand pointing in front. Right in the direction of my finger, he repeated.

The ticket collector had sat down on a bench near the railing. He had finished making his rounds and was watching their movements. Maybe he guessed what they were saying, because he went over to them, smiling, and spoke to the woman with an amused expression. She listened attentively, then exclaimed: Noooo!, and she brought a hand to her mouth with a mischievous, childish look, as though suppressing a laugh. What's he say? the man asked, with the slightly stolid expression of someone who can't follow a conversation. The woman gave the ticket collector a look of complicity. Her eyes were laughing and she was very attractive. He says they're not rocks, she said, deliberately holding back what she had learnt. The man looked at her, questioning and perhaps a little annoyed. They're small blue whales strolling about the Azores, she exclaimed, those are the exact words he used. And she at last let out the laugh she'd been holding back, a small, quick, ringing laugh. Suddenly her expression changed and she pushed back the hair the wind had blown across her face. You know at the airport I mistook someone else for you? she said, candidly revealing her association of ideas. He didn't even have the same build as you and he was wearing an extraordinary shirt you'd never put on, not even for Carnival, isn't it odd? The man made a gesture with his hand, butting in: I stayed behind in the hotel, you know, the deadline's getting closer and the script still needs going over. But the woman wouldn't let him interrupt. It must be because I've been thinking about you so much, she went on, and about these islands, the sun. She was speaking in what was almost a whisper now, as if to herself. I've done nothing all this time but think of you. It never stopped raining. I imagined you sitting on a beach. It's been too long, I think. The man took her hand. For me too, he said, but I haven't been to the beach much, the main thing I've been looking at is my typewriter. And then it rains here too, oh yes, you wouldn't believe the rain, how heavy it is. The woman smiled. I haven't even asked you if you've managed to do it, and to think, if ideas were worth anything, I'd have written ten plays myself with trying to imagine yours: tell me what it's like, I'm dying to know. Oh, let's say it's a reworking of Ibsen in a light vein, he said, without disguising a certain enthusiasm – light, but a little bitter too, the way my stuff is, and seen from her point of view. How do you mean? asked the woman. Oh, the man said with conviction, you know the way things are going these days I thought it would be wise to present it from her point of view, if I want people to take notice, even if that's not why I wrote it, of course. The story's banal in the end, a relationship breaking up, but all stories are banal, what matters is the point of view, and I rescue the woman, she is the real protagonist, he is selfish and mediocre, he doesn't even realise what he's losing, do you get me?

The woman nodded. I think so, she said, I'm not sure. In any case I've been writing some other stuff as well, he went on, these islands are a crushing bore, there's nothing to do to pass the time but write. And then I wanted to try my hand at a different genre. I've been writing fiction all my life. It seems nobler to me, the woman said, or at least more gratuitous, and hence, how can I put it, lighter . . . Oh right, laughed the man, delicacy: *par délicatesse j'ai perdu ma vie*. But there comes a time when you have to have the courage to try your hand at reality, at least the reality of our own lives. And then, listen, people can't get enough of real-life experience, they're tired of the imaginings of novelists of no imagination. Very softly the woman asked: are they memoirs? Her subdued voice quivered slightly with anxiety. Kind of, he said, but there's no elaboration of interpretation or memory; the bare facts and nothing more: that's what counts. It'll stir things up, said the woman. Let's say people will take notice, he corrected. The woman was silent for a moment, thoughtful. Do you already have a title, she asked. Maybe *Le regard sans école*, he said, what do you think? Sounds witty, she said.

Steering around in a wide curve, the boat began to sail along the coast of the island. Puffs of black smoke with a strong smell of diesel flew out of the funnel and the engine settled into a calm chug, as if enjoying itself. That's why it takes so long, the man said, the landing stage must be on the other side of the island.

You know, Marcel, the woman resumed, as if pursuing an idea of her own, I saw a lot of Albertine this winter. The boat proceeded in small lurches, as if the engine were jamming. They sailed by a little church right on the waterfront and they were so near they could almost make out the faces of the people going in. The bells summoning the faithful to Mass had a jarring sound, as though dragging their feet.

What?! The man chased the invisible insect from the tip of his nose. What on earth do you mean? he said. His face took on an expression of amazement and great disappointment. We kept each other company, she explained. A lot. It's important to keep each other company in life, don't you think? The man stood up and leaned on the railing, then sat on his seat again. But what do you mean, he repeated, have you gone mad? He seemed extremely restless, his legs couldn't keep still. She's an unhappy woman, and a generous one, the woman said, still following her own reasoning, I think she loved you a great deal. The man stretched out his arms in a disconsolate gesture and muttered something incomprehensible. Listen, forget it, he finally said with an effort, anyway look, we've arrived.

The boat was preparing to dock. At the stern two men in T-shirts were unrolling the mooring cable and shouting to a third man standing on the landing stage watching them with his hands on his hips. A small crowd of relatives had gathered to greet the passengers and were waving. In the front row were two old women with black headscarves and a girl dressed up as though for her first communion hopping on one foot.

And what about the play, the woman suddenly enquired, as if all at once remembering something she had meant to ask, do you have a title for the play? You didn't tell me. Her companion was sorting out some newspapers and a small camera in a bag that bore the logo of an airline company. I've thought of hundreds and rubbished them all, he said, still bending down over his bag, not one that's really right, you need a witty title for a thing like this but something that sounds really good too. He stood up and a vague expression of hope lit up in his eyes. Why? he asked. Oh nothing, she said, just asking; I was thinking of a possible title, but maybe it's too frivolous, it wouldn't sound right on a serious poster, and then it's got nothing to do with your subject matter, it would sound completely incongruous. Oh come on, he begged, at least you can satisfy my curiosity, maybe it's brilliant. Silly, she said, completely off target.

The passengers crowded around the gangway and Marcel was sucked into the crush. The woman stood apart, holding onto the cable of the railing. I'll wait for you on the wharf, he shouted, without turning, I've got to move with the crowd! He raised an arm above the gaggle of heads, waving his hand. She leaned on the railing and began to gaze at the sea.

Other Fragments

In April 1839 two British citizens disembarked on the island of Flores which, together with Corvo, is the most remote and isolated island of the Azores archipelago. It was curiosity had brought them there, always an excellent guide. They landed at Santa Cruz, a village situated at the northernmost point of the island and boasting a small natural port which still offers the safest place to land on Flores today. From Santa Cruz they set out to travel, on foot and by litter, around the coast as far as Lajes de Flores, about forty kilometres away, where they wanted to see a church that the Portuguese had built in the seventeenth century. The litter, borne on the shoulders of eight islanders, was made from a ship's sail and judging by the travellers' description would seem to have been little more than a hammock strung between two poles.

Like all the other islands of the archipelago, Flores is volcanic in origin, although unlike São Miguel or Faial, for example, which have white beaches and brilliant green woods, Flores is just one great slab of black lava in the midst of the ocean. Flowers grow well on volcanoes, as

Bécquer was to remark; the two Englishmen thus crossed an incredible landscape; a slab of flowering slate which would suddenly open up into fearful chasms, precipices, sheer cliffs falling to the sea. Halfway to their destination they stopped to spend the night in a little fishing village. It was a tiny settlement perched on top of a cliff and the travellers don't mention the name: not out of carelessness, I don't think, since their account is always precise and detailed, but perhaps because it had no name. Most likely it was simply called *Aldeia*, which means 'village', and being the only inhabited place for miles around this general term did perfectly well for a proper name. From a distance it seemed an attractive place with a tidy geometry, as little fishing villages often are. The houses, however, seemed to have bizarre shapes. When they got to the village they realised why. The fronts of almost all the houses had been made with the prows of sailing ships; they had a triangular floor plan, some were made with good hard woods, and the only stone wall was the one that closed the three sides of the triangle. Some of the houses were quite beautiful, the amazed Englishmen tell us, their interiors scarcely looking like houses at all since almost all the furnishings – lanterns, seats, tables and even beds – had been taken from the sea. Many had portholes for windows and since they looked out over the precipice and the sea below they gave the impression of being in a sailing ship which has landed on top of a mountain. These houses were built with the remains of the shipwrecks into which over the centuries the rocks of Flores and Corvo had enticed passing ships. The Englishmen were offered hospitality in a house whose façade bore in white letters the legend: THE PLYMOUTH BALTIMORE, which perhaps helped them feel almost at home. And indeed they woke up refreshed the following morning and resumed their journey in the sail.

The two travellers were called Joseph and Henry Bullar and their journey deserves a mention.

In November 1838 a London doctor, Joseph Bullar, having already tried, without success, all the then known treatments for consumption on his brother Henry, decided, when Henry's condition deteriorated, to make a voyage with him to the island of São Miguel. Despite the distance and its extraordinary isolation, São Miguel, of all Atlantic islands with a warm climate, was the only one which could guarantee regular communications with England. During the orange season, that is from November to May, you could send a letter to England every week and receive a reply after three weeks, since the ship that carried oranges to England also offered a postal service. In those days São Miguel was one enormous orange orchard from coast to coast, with the trees running right down to the shore.

After a fairly rough voyage on the orange ship, the two brothers arrived at Ponta Delgada in December 1838 and stayed in São Miguel until

April 1839. One can assume that Henry's health benefited somewhat, since on leaving the main island the two brothers decided to set out in small fishermen's sailing boats to visit the central and western Azores. Their time in the archipelago, and particularly in Faial, Pico, and the remote Corvo, produced a splendid travel diary which once back in London the Bullar brothers published at John van Voorst's printing press in 1841, under the title *A Winter in the Azores and a Summer at the Furnas*. One reads it today with admiration and amazement, though when all is said and done things on the Azores have not changed so very much.

Almas or *alminhas*: souls and little souls. A cross on a square stone block with a blue-and-white tile in the middle depicting St Michael. The souls appear on 2 November when St Michael fishes them out of purgatory with a rope. He needs a rope for every soul. São Miguel is full of crosses, and hence of souls who haunt the reefs, the precipices, the lava beaches where the sea lashes. Late at night or very early in the morning, if you listen carefully you can hear their voices. Confused wailing, litanies, whispers, which the sceptical or distracted may easily mistake for the noise of the sea or the crying of the vultures. Many are the souls of shipwrecked sailors.

The first ships of the Portuguese explorers broke up here, the pirate ships of Sir Walter Raleigh and

the Earl of Cumberland, the Spanish fleet of Don
Pedro de Valdez who wanted to annex the Azores
to King Philip's crown. Actually the Spanish did
manage to disembark and their ruin wasn't
complete until the battle of Salga fought on
Terceira in 1581. The islanders waited for the
Spanish army on top of a hill, then drove herds of
crazed bulls down to rout the invaders. Among
the Spanish were Cervantes and Lope de Vega,
who described the savage battle in a quatrain.

Then came the fashionable shipwrecks which
made the headlines in newspapers and maga-
zines. The vicissitudes of rich, bizarre travellers
who had themselves photographed on their
luxury yachts as they set sail from New York or
New Bedford. Platinum blonde curls in the
breeze, blazers with gold buttons, silk scarves.
The champagne cork pops and the wine froths
out of the bottle. One thinks of foxtrots and
other dance music. The names of the boats
are as whimsical as the lives of their owners:
Ho Ho, *Anahita*, *Banana Split*. Bon voyage, sirs,
announces some minor local politician come
to cut the mooring line with silver scissors.
    The world is on the rocks too, but they don't
seem to notice.

At the end of the nineteenth century Albert I,
Prince of Monaco, sailed by these islands on
board his *Hirondelle*. It was in these seas that he
carried out many of his excellent oceanographic

studies, descended into the deepest waters in his pressure suit, catalogued unknown molluscs, strange life-forms with vague, uncertain shapes, fish and seaweeds. He left some very lively pages on the Azores, but what struck me most of all was his description of the death of a sperm-whale, a gigantic animal whose doom is as majestic and terrifying as the wreck of a transatlantic liner.

In order to observe the normal guidelines of the maritime authorities, the whalers move quickly to tow the sperm-whale's carcass out to sea, since its decomposition would otherwise rapidly contaminate the whole surrounding area. It is not an easy task, for although it might seem sufficient to drag the carcass two or three hundred metres from the shore and rely on a favourable current to carry it away. the capricious wind can always bring it back; sometimes the whalers will struggle in vain to be rid of the stinking hulk for days and days. Then if the sea gets rough, the undesirable carrion may well be trapped by the waves beneath inaccessible cliffs whence its heavy stench will for months and months constitute a torment to the inhabitants of the region. Finally, one hot sunny day, the large intestine, blown up with gas, will explode with a boom, covering the surrounding area with bits of offal which constitute a delicious food for the multicoloured scavenger crabs. Sometimes these sinister creatures arrange to meet for their foul five o'clock tiffin with elegant shrimps which parade their delicate antennae over the enormous cake, always given that the high tide is so kind as to offer the latter a means of transport. But whatever the details, the fact remains that the poor sperm-whale proceeds along the road of his ruin from the first wound inflicted on him by man right through to the action of the humble creatures who take him to the completion of that fatal cycle which is the destiny of every living being. The death of a sperm-whale is as majestic as the crumbling of a great building, and in the necropoli set up by the whalers in the little bays, the animal's remains pile up like the broken walls of a cathedral.

For a long time I carried around in my memory a phrase of Chateaubriand's: *Inutile phare de la nuit*. I believe I always attributed to these words the power of comfort in disenchantment: as when we attach ourselves to something that turns out to be an *inutile phare de la nuit*, yet nevertheless allows us to do something merely because we believed in its light: the power of illusions. In my memory this phrase was associated with the name of a distant and improbable island: *Ile de Pico, inutile phare de la nuit*.

When I was fifteen I read *Les Natchez*, an incongruous, absurd and in its way magnificent book. It was the gift of an uncle who for the whole of his short life cultivated the dream of becoming an actor and who probably loved Chateaubriand for his theatricality and scene painting. The book fascinated me, took my imagination by the hand and drew it with irresist- ible force through the stage curtains of adventure. I remember some passages of the book by heart and for years I thought that the phrase about the beacon belonged to it. Then it occurred to me to quote the exact passage in this notebook, so I re-read *Les Natchez*, but couldn't find my phrase. At first I thought it had escaped me because I had re-read the book with the haste of one who is merely looking for a quote. Then I realised that not finding a phrase like this partakes of the most intimate sense of the phrase itself, and this was a consolation for me. I also wondered what part the perhaps unconscious forces of evocation and suggestion generated by this phrase might have played in calling me to an island where there was nothing to attract me. Sometimes the directions we take in our lives can be decided by the combination of a few words.

I need only add that on Pico at night no beacons shone.

Breezy and Rupert invite me onto their boat for a farewell drink. They are leaving in the afternoon, since in order to get away from the island they want to take advantage of the seven o'clock calm, a phenomenon which exists here as elsewhere. Moored opposite the water tanks, the *Amadeus* is blue and white, rocking gently, and it seems impossible to me that such a small boat is capable of crossing oceans.

Rupert has very red hair, freckles, an amusing, Danny Kaye-like face. Perhaps he told me he was Scottish, or perhaps I just think of him as such because of his face. He used to work in a shipping company in London: years and years sitting at a table under electric light, dreaming of the distant ports whence the company's exotic merchandise arrived. So one day he handed in his notice, sold what he had, and bought this boat. Or rather, he had it custom-built to the design of a New York boat architect. And when I go below on the *Amadeus* I appreciate it isn't quite the fragile eggshell it seems when you see it from the land. Breezy came with him and they live together on the boat. Welcome to our home, they say laughing. Breezy has an open, very friendly face, a marvellous smile, and she's wearing a long flowery dress as if preparing for a garden party, not a transatlantic crossing. The interior is furnished with hard woods and warm-coloured upholsteries which immediately convey a feeling of comfort and safety. There is a small, well-stocked library. I begin to browse: Melville, of course, and Conrad and Stevenson. But there is Henry James too, and Kipling, Shaw, Wells, *Dubliners*, Somerset Maugham, Forster, Joyce Cary, H. E. Bates. I pick up *The Jacaranda Tree* and inevitably the conversation turns to Brazil. They have only been as far as Fortaleza do Ceará, sailing down the coasts of America. But they are saving Brazil for another trip; first Rupert has to arrange to rent out the *Amadeus* for a small luxury cruise. That's how they live, renting out the boat, and usually Rupert stays on board and sails it. The rest of their life is all their own.

We lift our glasses and drink to their trip. May fair winds follow you, I toast, now and always.

Rupert slides back the door of a shelf and slips a tape into the stereo. It is Mozart's Concerto K 271 for piano and orchestra, and only now do I realise why the boat is called *Amadeus*. The shelf contains the complete works of Mozart on tape, catalogued with meticulous care. I think of Rupert and Breezy crossing the seas to the accompaniment of Mozart's tunes and harpsichords, and for me the idea has a strange beauty to it, perhaps because I have always associated music with the idea of terra firma, of the concert hall or a cosy room in the half-dark. The music takes on a solemn sound and draws us in. The glasses are empty, we get up and embrace each other. Rupert starts the engine, I climb onto the steps and with a jump am down on the wharf. There's a soft light on the circle of houses which is Porto Pim. *Amadeus* turns in a wide curve and sets off at speed. Breezy is at the helm and Rupert is hoisting the sail. I stand there waving until *Amadeus*, all its sails already unfurled, reaches the open sea.

When sailors stop at Horta it is a custom to leave a drawing with name and date on the wall of the wharf. The wall is a hundred metres long and drawings of boats, flag colours, numbers and graffiti are all jumbled up one on top of the other. I record one of the many: 'Nat, from Brisbane. I go where the wind takes me.'

In July 1895, the winds brought Captain Joshua Slocum as far as Horta. Slocum was the first man to sail solo around the world. His yacht was called

Spray and the impression you get from photographs is of a tub of a boat, clumsy and unstable, better suited for river sailing than a trip around the world. Captain Slocum left some quite beautiful pages on the Azores. I read them in his *Sailing Alone around the World*, an old old edition, the cover decorated with a festoon of anchors.

The winds also brought the only woman whaler I ever heard of to the Azores. Her name was Miss Elisa Nye. She was seventeen years old and to reach her maternal grandfather, the naturalist Thomas Hickling, who had invited her to spend a year with him in his house in São Miguel, she thought nothing of boarding a whaler, the *Sylph*, which was travelling under sail from New Bedford to the Western Isles, as the Americans then called the Azores. Miss Elisa was a bright, enterprising girl, brought up in an American family of frugal and puritan traditions. She wasn't discouraged by life on the whaler and did her best to make herself useful. Her trip lasted from 10 July to 13 August 1847. In her engaging diary, written with freshness and dispatch, she talks of the sea, of old Captain Garner, gruff and fatherly, the dolphins, the sharks, and, of course, the whales. In her free time, apart from keeping up her diary, she read the Bible and Byron's *The Corsair*.

Peter's Bar is a café on the dockside at Horta, near the sailing club. It is a cross between a tavern, a meeting point, an information agency and a post office. The whalers go there, but so too do the yachting folks crossing the Atlantic or making other long trips. And since the sailors know that Faial is an obligatory stopover point and that everybody passes through, Peter's has become the forwarding address for precarious and hopeful messages that otherwise would have no destination. On the wooden counter at Peter's the proprietor pins notes, telegrams, letters, which wait for someone to come and claim them. 'For Regina, Peter's Bar, Horta, Azores', says an envelope with a Canadian stamp. 'Pedro e Pilar Vazquez Cuesta, Peter's Bar, Azores': the letter was mailed in Argentina and has arrived just the same. A slightly yellowed note says: *'Tom, excuse-moi, je suis partie pour le Brésil, je ne pouvais plus rester ici, je devenais folle. Écris-moi, viens, je t'attends. C/o Engenheiro Silveira Martins, Avenida Atlântica 3025, Copacabana. Brigitte.'* Another implores: 'Notice. To boats bound for Europe. Crew available!!! I am 24, with 26,000 miles of crewing/cruising/cooking experience. If you have room for one more, please leave word below! Carol Shepard.'

She's slim, very streamlined, built of top quality material. She must have been around a great deal. She arrived in this port by chance. But then journeys are a chance. She's called *Nota azzurra*.

*

Mountains of fire, wind and solitude: thus, in the sixteenth century did one of the first Portuguese travellers to land here describe the Azores.

Antero de Quental
A Life

Antero was born the last of nine children into a large Azores family which possessed both pastureland and orange orchards, and so grew up amid the austere and frugal affluence of island landowners. Among his forebears were an astronomer and a mystic, whose portraits, together with that of his grandfather, adorned the walls of a dark sitting room which smelt of camphor. His grandfather had been called André da Ponte Quental and had suffered exile and prison for having taken part in the first liberal revolution in 1820. So much his father told him, a kind man who loved horses and had fought in the battle of Mindelo against the absolutists.

To keep him company in his early years he had some small dappled colts and the archaic lullabies of serving women who came down from the mountains of São Miguel where the villages are built of lava and have names like Caldeiras and Pico do Ferro. He was a calm pale child, with reddish hair and eyes so clear they sometimes seemed transparent. He spent the mornings in the patio of a solid house where the women kept the keys to the cupboards and the windows had curtains made from thick lace. He ran about letting out little whoops of joy and was happy. He was particularly close to his oldest brother, whose singular and bizarre intelligence would for long periods be overshadowed by a silent madness. Together they invented a game called 'Heaven and Earth' with cobblestones and shells for pieces, playing on a circular chequerboard sketched in the dust.

When the child was of an age to learn, his father called the Portuguese poet Feliciano de Castilho to their house and entrusted him with the boy's education. At the time Castilho was considered a great poet, perhaps because of his versions of Ovid and Goethe and perhaps again because of the misfortune of his blindness which sometimes conferred on his poetry that prophetic tone beloved of the Romantics. In fact he was a peevish, crusty scholar with a preference for rhetoric and grammar. With him the young Antero learnt Latin, German and metrics. And amidst these studies he reached adolescence.

On the April night of his fifteenth birthday, Antero woke up with a start and felt that he must go down to the sea. It was a calm night with a waxing moon. The whole household was asleep and the wind bellied the lace curtains. He dressed in silence and went down toward the cliffs. He sat on a rock and looked at the sky, trying to imagine what could have prompted him to come here. The sea was calm and breathed as though asleep, and the night was like any other night. Just that he had a great sense of disquiet, of anxiety weighing on his chest. And at that moment he heard a dull bellow rising from the earth, the moon turned blood red and the sea swelled up like an enormous belly to crash down on the rocks. The earth shook and the trees bent under the force of a rushing wind. Antero ran home bewildered to find the family gathered together in the patio; but the danger was over now and the women's embarrassment at being seen in their nightclothes was already greater than the fright they had suffered. Before going back to bed, Antero took a piece of paper and, unable to control himself, wrote down some words. And as he wrote he became aware that the words were arranging themselves on the page, by themselves almost, in the form and metre of a sonnet: and he dedicated it, in Latin, to the unknown god who was inspiring him. That night he slept soundly and at dawn dreamt that a small monkey with a sad ironic little face was offering him a note. He read the note and discovered a secret no one else had been allowed to know, except the monkey.

He approached manhood. He studied astronomy and geometry, he came under the spell of Laplace's cosmogony, of the idea of a unity of physical forces and a mathematical conception of space. In the evening he wrote descriptions of mysterious, abstract little contrivances, translating into words his idea of the cosmic machine. By now he had resigned himself to his dreams of the small monkey with the sad ironic little face and was amazed those nights when the creature did not visit him.

When he reached university age he left for Coimbra as family tradition required and announced that the moment had come for him to give up his studies of cosmic laws and dedicate himself to the laws of man. He was now a tall solid boy with a blond beard that gave him a majestic, almost arrogant look. In Coimbra he discovered love, read Michelet and Proudhon and instead of studying the laws used to apply the justice of the time, got excited by the idea of a new justice based on the equality and dignity of man. He pursued this idea with the passion he had inherited from his island forebears, but likewise with the reason of the man he was, for he was convinced that justice and equality formed part of the geometry of the world. In the perfect, closed form of the sonnet, he expressed the ardour that possessed him and his eagerness for truth. He left for Paris and became a typesetter, the way someone else might have become a monk, because he wanted to experience physical tiredness and the concreteness of manual tools. After France he went to England and then the USA, living in New York and Halifax, so as to get to know the new metropolises man was building and the different ways of life they engendered. By the time he went back to Portugal he had become a socialist. He founded the National Association of Workers, travelled and made converts, lived among the peasants, passed through his own islands with the fiery oratory of the demagogue; he came up against the arrogance of the powerful, the flattery of the sly, the cowardliness of servants. He was animated by disdain and wrote sonnets full of sarcasm and fury. He also experienced the betrayal of certain comrades and the ambiguous alchemy of those who manage to combine the common good with their own advantage.

He realised he would have to leave it to others more able than himself to press on with the work he had begun, almost as though that work no longer belonged to him. The time had come for practical men, and he was not practical. This filled him with a sense of desolation, like a child who loses his innocence and suddenly discovers how vulgar the world is. He wasn't even fifty yet and his face was deeply scored. The eyes had sunk into hollows and his beard was going grey. He began to suffer from insomnia and in the rare moments when he did sleep would let out low muffled cries. Sometimes he had the impression his words did not belong to him and often to his surprise he would catch himself talking out loud alone as if he were somebody else talking to himself, Antero. A Parisian doctor diagnosed hysteria and prescribed electric shock therapy. In a note Antero wrote that he was suffering from 'the infinite', and perhaps in his case this was the more plausible explanation. Perhaps he was just tired of this transitory, imperfect form of the ideal and of passion, his yearning now taking him toward another kind of geometrical order. In his writings, the word Nothing began to appear, seeming to him now the most perfect form of perfection. In his forty-ninth year he returned to his native island.

The morning of 11 September 1891 he left his house in Ponta Delgada, walked quickly down the steep shady road to Igreja Matriz and went into a small shop on the corner that sold arms. He was wearing a black suit and white shirt, his tie fixed with a tiepin made with a shell. The shopkeeper was a friendly, obese man who loved dogs and old prints. A bronze fan turned slowly on the ceiling. The owner showed his customer a beautiful seventeenth-century print he had recently bought depicting a pack of dogs chasing a stag. The old shopkeeper had been a friend of his father's and Antero remembered how, as a child, the two men had taken him to the Caloura fair which boasted the best horses in São Miguel. They talked for a long time about dogs and horses, then Antero bought a small revolver with a short barrel. When he left the shop the bell-tower of Matriz was striking eleven. He walked slowly along by the sea as far as the harbour office, and stood a long time on the wharf looking out at the clippers. Then he crossed the coast road and walked into the circle of gaunt plane trees around Praça da Esperança. The sun was fierce and everything was white. The *praça* was deserted at that time of day, because of the extreme heat. A sad-looking donkey, tied to a ring on a wall, let his head loll. As he was crossing the square, Antero caught the sound of music. He stopped and turned. In the opposite corner, under the shade of a plane tree, a tramp was playing a barrel organ. The tramp nodded and Antero walked over to him. He was a lean gipsy and he had a monkey on his shoulder. It was a small animal with a sad, ironic little face, wearing a red uniform with gold buttons. Antero recognised the monkey of his dreams and realised who it was. The animal held out its tiny black hand and Antero dropped a coin in it. In exchange the monkey pulled out one of the many slips of coloured paper the gypsy kept tucked in the ribbon of his hat and offered it to him. He took it and read it. He crossed the *praça* and sat on a bench under the cool wall of the Esperança convent where a blue anchor had been painted on the whitewash. He took the revolver from his pocket, brought it to his mouth and pulled the trigger. For a moment he was amazed to find he was still seeing the *praça*, the trees, the sparkle of the sea, the gypsy playing his barrel organ. He felt a warm trickle running down his neck. He clicked the drum of the revolver and fired again. At which the gypsy disappeared along with the rest of the scene and the bells of Matriz began to strike twelve noon.

II

Of Whales and Whalemen

High Seas

Towards the end of the last war an exhausted and perhaps sick whale ran aground on the beach of a small German town, I don't know which. Like the whale, Germany too was exhausted and sick, the town had been destroyed and the people were hungry. The inhabitants of the little town went to the beach to see this giant visitor who lay there in forced and unnatural immobility, and breathed. A few days went by, but the whale didn't die. Every day the people went to look at the whale. No one in the town knew how to kill an animal which wasn't an animal but a huge dark, polished cylinder they had previously seen only in illustrations. Until one day someone took a big knife, went up to the whale, carved out a cone of oily flesh and hurried home with it. The whole population began to carve away pieces of the whale. They went at night, in secret, because they were ashamed to be seen, even though they knew everybody was doing the same thing. The whale went on living for many days, despite being riddled with horrific wounds.

My friend Christoph Meckel told me this story some time ago. I thought I had got it out of my mind, but it came back to me all at once when I got off the boat on the island of Pico and there was a dead whale floating near the rocks.

When whales float in the middle of the ocean they look like drifting submarines struck by torpedoes. And in their bellies one imagines a crew of lots of little Jonahs whose radar is out of operation and who have given up trying to contact other Jonahs and are awaiting their deaths with resignation.

I read in a scientific review that whales use ultrasound to communicate with each other. They have extremely fine hearing and can pick up each other's calls hundreds of kilometres away. Once herds would communicate with each other from the most distant parts of the globe. Usually they were mating calls or other kinds of messages whose meaning we don't understand. Now that the seas are full of mechanical noises and artificial ultrasound, the whales' messages suffer such interference that other whales can no longer pick them up and decipher them. In vain they go on transmitting calls and signals which wander about lost in the depths of the sea.

There is a position whales assume which fishermen describe as the 'dead whale' pose. It is almost always the adult and isolated whale which does this. When 'dead', the whale appears to have abandoned itself completely to the surface of the sea, rising and falling without any apparent effort, as though in the grip of a deep sleep. Fishermen claim that this phenomenon only occurs on days of intense heat or with dead calm seas, but the real reasons for the cetaceous catalepsy are unknown.

Whalemen maintain that whales are entirely indifferent to a human presence even when they are copulating, and that they will let people get so close as to be able to touch them. The sex act takes place by pressing belly to belly, as in the human species. Whalemen say that while mating the heads of the pair come out of the water, but naturalists maintain that whales assume a horizontal position and that the vertical position is just a product of the fishermen's imagination.

Our knowledge of the birth of whales and the first moments of their lives is likewise fairly limited. In any event something different from what we know goes on with other marine mammals must happen to prevent the young whale from being drowned or suffocated when the umbilical cord linking it to the mother's vascular system breaks. As is well known, birth and copulation are the only moments in the lives of other marine mammals when they seem to remember their terrestrial origins. Thus they come ashore only to mate and give birth, staying just long enough for the young to survive the first phases of their life. Of all terrestrial acts, this then should be the last to fade from the physiological memory of the whale, which of all aquatic mammals is the furthest from its terrestrial origins.

'No relationship exists between this gentle race of mammals, who like ourselves have red blood and milk, and the monsters of the previous age, horrible abortions of the primordial slime. Far more recent, the whale found cleansed water, an open sea and a peaceful earth. The milk of the sea and its oil abounded; its warm fat, animalised, seethed with extraordinary strength, it wanted to live. These elements fermented together and formed themselves into great giants, *enfants gâtés* of a nature which endowed them with incomparable strength and, more precious yet: fine fire-red blood. For the first time blood appeared on the scene. Here was the true flower of this world. All the creatures with pale, mean, languid, vegetating blood seem utterly without heart when compared to the generous life that boils up in this porpoise whether in anger or love. The strength of the higher world, its charm, its beauty, is blood . . . But with this magnificent gift nervous sensibility is likewise infinitely increased. One is far more vulnerable, has far more capacity to suffer and to enjoy. Since the whale has absolutely no sense of the hunt, and its senses of smell and hearing are not very highly developed, everything is entrusted to touch. The fat which defends the whale from the cold does not protect it from knocks at all. Finely arranged in six separate tissues, the skin trembles and quivers at every contact. The tender papillae which cover the whale are the instruments of a most delicate sense of touch. And all this is animated, brought to life by a gush of red blood, which given the massive size of the animal is not even remotely comparable in terms of abundance to the blood of terrestrial mammals. A wounded whale floods the sea in a moment, dyes it red across a huge distance. The blood which we have in drops has been poured into the whale in torrents.

'The female carries her young for nine months. Her tasty rather sugary milk has the warm sweetness of a woman's. But since the whale must always forge through the waves, if the udders were located on the breast, the young whale would be constantly exposed to the brunt of the sea; hence they are to be found a little further down, in a more sheltered place, on the belly, whence the young whale was born. And the baby hides away there and takes pleasure in the wave that his mother breaks for him.' (Michelet, *La Mer*, page 238)

They say that ambergris is formed from the remains of the keratin shells of shellfish that the whale is unable to digest and which accumulate in certain segments of the intestine. But others maintain that it forms as the result of a pathological process, a sort of limited intestinal calculus. Today ambergris is used almost exclusively in the production of luxury perfumes, but in the past it had as many applications as human fantasy could dream up for it: it was used as a propitiatory balsam in religious rites, as an aphrodisiac lotion, and as a sign of religious dedication for Muslim pilgrims visiting the Qa'aba in Mecca. It is said to have been an indispensable aperitif at the banquets of the Mandarins. Milton talks about ambergris in *Paradise Lost*. Shakespeare mentions it too, I don't remember where.

'L'amour, chez eux, soumis à des conditions difficiles, veut un lieu de profonde paix. Ainsi que le noble éléphant, qui craint les yeux profanes, la baleine n'aime qu'au désert. Le rendez-vous est vers les pôles, aux anses solitaires du Groënland, aux brouillards de Behring, sans doute aussi dans la mer tiède qu'on a trouvée près du pôle même.

'La solitude est grande. C'est un théâtre étrange de mort et de silence pour cette fête de l'ardente vie. Un ours blanc, un phoque, un renard bleu peut-être, témoins respectueux, prudents, observent à distance. Les lustres et girandoles, les miroirs fantastiques, ne manquent pas. Cristaux bleuâtres, pics, aigrettes de glace éblouissante, neiges vierges, ce sont les témoins qui siègent tout autour et regardent.

'Ce qui rend cet hymen touchant et grave, c'est qu'il y faut l'expresse volonté. Ils n'ont pas l'arme tyrannique du requin, ces attaches qui maîtrisent le plus faible. Au contraire, leurs fourreaux glissants les séparent, les éloignent. Ils se fuient

malgré eux, échappent, par ce désespérant obstacle. Dans un si grand accord, on dirait un
combat. Des baleiniers prétendent avoir vu ce
spectacle unique. Les amants, d'un brûlant transport, par instants, dressés et debout, comme les
deux tours de Notre-Dame, gémissant de leurs
bras trop courts, entreprenaient de s'embrasser.
Ils retombaient d'un poids immense . . . L'ours et
l'homme fuyaient épouvantés de leurs soupirs'
(Michelet, *La Mer*, pages 240–42). So intense
and poetic is this passage from Michelet it would
be wrong to tone it down with a translation.

Those days of intense sunshine and oppressive
stillness when a thick sultry heat weighs on the
ocean – it occurred to me these might be the rare
moments when whales return in their physiological memory to their terrestrial origins. To do
this they have to concentrate so intensely and
completely that they fall into a deep sleep which
gives an appearance of death: and thus floating
on the surface, like blind, polished stumps, they
somehow remember, as though in a dream, a
distant, distant past when their clumsy fins were
dry limbs capable of gestures, greetings, caresses,
races through the grass amid tall flowers and
ferns, on an earth that was a magma of elements
still in search of a combination, an idea.

The whalemen of the Azores will tell you that
when an adult whale is harpooned at a distance of
five or six miles from another, the latter, even if in

this state of apparent death, will wake with a start and flee in fear. The whales hunted in the Azores are mainly sperm-whales.

'*Sperm Whale*. This whale, among the English of old vaguely known as the Trumpa Whale, and the Physeter Whale, and the Anvil Headed Whale, is the present Cachalot of the French, and the Pottfisch of the Germans, and the Macrocephalus of the Long Words. He is, without doubt, the largest inhabitant of the globe; the most formidable of all whales to encounter; the most majestic in aspect; and lastly, by far the most valuable in commerce; he being the only creature from which that valuable substance, spermaceti, is obtained. All his peculiarities will, in many other places, be enlarged upon. It is chiefly with his name that I now have to do. Philologically considered, it is absurd. Some centuries ago, when the Sperm Whale was almost wholly unknown in his own proper individuality, and when his oil was only accidentally obtained from the stranded fish; in those days spermaceti, it would seem, was popularly supposed to be derived from a creature identical with the one then known in England as the Greenland or Right Whale. It was the idea also, that this same spermaceti was that quickening humor of the Greenland Whale which the first syllable of the word literally expresses. In those times, also, spermaceti was exceedingly scarce, not being used for light, but only as an ointment and medicament. It was only to be had from the druggists as you nowadays buy an ounce of rhubarb. When, as I opine, in the course of time, the true nature of spermaceti became known, its original name was still retained by the dealers; no doubt to enhance its value by a notion so strangely significant of its scarcity.' (Melville, *Moby Dick*, chapter XXXII)

'Sperm-whales are great whales which live in areas of both hemispheres where the water temperature is fairly high. There are important differences between their physiology and that of other whales: the whalebones which fortify the mouth of the latter and which are used to grind up small elements of food, are replaced in the sperm-whale by sturdy teeth firmly inserted in the lower jaw and capable of snapping a large prey; the head, an enormous mass which ends vertically like the prow of a ship, accounts for a third of the whole body. These anatomical differences between the two groups of whales assign them to distinct territories: other whales find the thick banks of microscopic organisms they feed on mainly in the cold waters of the polar regions where they absorb this food with the same naturalness with which we breathe; the sperm-whale, on the other hand, mainly feeds on cephalopods which flourish in temperate waters. There are also important differences in the way these giant whales behave, differences which whalemen have learnt to recognise to perfection in the interests of their own safety. While other whales are peaceful animals, the older male sperm-whale, like the boar, lives alone and will both defend and avenge himself. Having wounded the creature with their harpoons, many whaleboats have been snatched between the jaws of these giants and then crushed to pieces; and many crews have perished in the hunt.' (Albert i, Prince of Monaco, *La Carrière d'un Navigateur*, pages 277–78)

'No small number of these whaling seamen belong to the Azores, where the outward bound Nantucket whalers frequently touch to augment their crews from the hardy peasants of those rocky shores . . . How it is, there is no telling, but Islanders seem to make the best whalemen.' (Melville, *Moby Dick*, chapter XXVII)

The island of Pico is a volcanic cone which rises sheer from the ocean: it is no more and no less than a high rocky mountain resting on the water. There are three villages: Madalena, São Roque and Lajes; the rest is lava rock on which are dotted meagre vineyards and a few wild pine-apples. The small ferry ties up at the landing stage in Madalena. It's Sunday and many families are taking trips to the nearby islands with baskets and bundles. The baskets are overflowing with pineapples, bananas, bottles of wine, fish. In Lajes there is a small whale museum I want to see. But since it's not a workday the bus isn't running very often and Lajes is forty kilometres away at the other end of the island. I sit patiently on a bench under a palm in front of the strange church that stands in the little *praça*. I planned to take a swim, it's a fine day and the temperature is pleasant. But on the ferry they told me to be careful, there's a dead whale near the rocks and the sea is full of sharks.

After a long wait in the midday heat I see a taxi which, having set down a passenger by the harbour, is turning back. The driver offers me a free ride to Lajes, because he has just made the trip and is going home; the price his passenger paid included the return trip and he doesn't want any money he doesn't deserve. There are only two taxis in Lajes, he tells me with a satisfied look, his and his cousin's. Pico's only road runs along the cliffs with bends and potholes above a foaming sea. It's a narrow, bumpy road crossing a grim stony landscape with just the occasional isolated house. I get off at the main square in Lajes, a quiet village dominated by an incongruously large eighteenth-century monastery and an imposing *padrão* – the stone monument that Portuguese sailors used to set up wherever they landed as a sign of their king's sovereignty.

The whale museum is in the main street on the first floor of a handsome renovated townhouse. My guide is a youngster with a vaguely half-witted air and a hackneyed, formal way of talking. What interests me most are the pieces of whale ivory which the whalemen used to carve, and then the ships' logs and some archaic tools of

141

bizarre design. Along one wall are some old photographs. One bears the caption: *Lajes, 25 de Dezembro 1919*. Heaven knows how they managed to drag the sperm-whale as far as the church. It must have taken quite a few pairs of oxen. It's a frighteningly huge sperm-whale, it seems incredible. Six or seven young boys have climbed up onto its head: they've placed a ladder against the front of the head and are waving caps and handkerchiefs on top. The whalemen are lined up in the foreground with a proud, satisfied air. Three of them are wearing woollen bobble caps, one has an oilskin hat shaped like a fireman's. They are all barefoot, only one has boots, he must be the master. I imagine they then left the photograph, took off their caps and went into church, as if it were the most natural thing in the world to leave a whale in the square outside. Thus they spent Christmas day on Pico in 1919.

As I come out of the museum, a surprise awaits me. From the end of the street, still deserted, appears a band. They are old men and boys dressed in white with sailors' caps, their brass buttons brightly polished and winking in the sun. They're playing a melancholy air, a waltz it seems, and they play it beautifully. In front of them walks a little girl holding a staff on the end of which two bread rolls and a dove made of sugar have been skewered. I follow the little procession in their lonely parade along the main street as far as a house with blue windows. The band arranges itself in a semicircle and strikes up a dashing march. A window opens and an old man with a distinguished look to him greets them, leaning out, smiling. He disappears, then reappears a moment later on the doorstep. He is met with a short burst of applause, a handshake from the bandleader, a kiss from the little girl. Obviously this is a homage, though to whom or what I don't know, and there wouldn't be much sense in asking. The very short ceremony is over, the band rearranges itself into two lines, but instead of turning back they set off toward the sea which is right there at the bottom of the street. They start playing again and I follow them. When they reach the sea they sit on the rocks, put their instruments down on the ground and light up cigarettes. They chat and look at the sea. They're enjoying their Sunday. The girl has left her staff leaning against a lamp-post and is playing with a friend her own age. From the other end of the village the bus honks its horn, because at six it will be making its only trip to Madalena, and right now it's five to.

'There are two sorts of whalemen in the Azores. The first come from the United States on small schooners of around a hundred tons. They look like pirate crews, because of the motley of races they include: negroes, Malays, Chinese and indefinable cosmopolitan crosses of this or that, are all mixed up with deserters and rascals using the ocean as a means of escape from the justice of men. An enormous boiler takes up the centre of the schooner; it is here that the chunks of lubber cut from the captured sperm-whale, which is tied to scaffolding beside the ship's hull, are transformed into oil using an infernal cooking process constantly disturbed by the pitch and roll of the boat: meanwhile coils of sickening smoke wreath all about. And when the sea is rough what a wild spectacle it becomes! Rather than give up the fruits of a prey heroically snatched from the belly of the Ocean, these men prefer to put their lives in jeopardy. To double the ropes holding the whale to the scaffolding, a number of men will risk their lives climbing out on that enormous oily mass awash with rushing water, its great bulk tossed about by the waves and threatening to smash the hull of the schooner to pieces. Having doubled the ropes they will hang on, prolonging the risk to the point where it is no longer tolerable. Then they cut the hawsers and the whole crew shouts violent angry imprecations at the carcass as it drifts off on the waves, leaving only a terrible stench where before it had inspired dreams of riches.

'The other group of whalemen is made up of people more similar to common mortals. They are the fishermen of the islands, or even adventurous farmers, and sometimes simple emigrants who have come back to their own country, their souls tempered by other storms in the Americas. Ten of them will get together to make up the crews for two whaling boats belonging to a tiny company with a capital of around thirty thous-

and francs. A third of the profits go to the share-holders, the other two thirds are divided equally between the members of the crews. The whaling sloops are admirably built for speed and fitted with sails, oars, paddles, an ordinary rudder and an oar-rudder. The hunting tools include several harpoons (their points carefully protected in cases), a number of fairly sharp steel lances, and five or six hundred metres of rope arranged in spirals inside baskets from which it runs forward through an upright fork on the prow of the boat.

'These small boats lie in wait, concealed on small beaches or in the rocky bays of these in-hospitable little islands. From a highpoint on the island a look-out constantly scans the sea the way a topman does on a ship; and when that column of watery steam the sperm-whale blows out from his spiracle is sighted, the look-out musters the whale-men with an agreed signal. In a few minutes the boats have taken to the sea and are heading towards the place where the drama will be con-summated.' (Albert I, Prince of Monaco, *La Carrière d'un Navigateur*, pages 280–83)

From a Code of Regulations

1   *Concerning the Whales*

Art. 1.   These regulations are valid for the hunt-ing of those whales indicated below when hunting is carried out in the territorial waters of Portugal and of the islands over which Portugal holds sovereignty:

Sperm-whale, *Physeter catodon* (Linnaeus)
Common Whale, *Baloenoptera physalus* (Linnaeus)
Blue Whale, *Baloenoptera musculus* (Linnaeus)
Dwarf Whale, *Baloenoptera acustorostrata*
   (Linnaeus)
Hump-backed Whale or 'Ampebeque', *Megaptera nodosa* (Linnaeus)

2   *Concerning the Boats*

Art. 2.   The craft used in the hunt shall be as follows:

a) *Whaling sloops.* Boats without decks, propelled by oar or sail, used in the hunt, that is to harpoon or kill the whales.

b) *Launches.* Mechanically propelled boats used to assist the whaling sloops by towing them and the whales killed. When necessary and within the terms of these regulations, such boats may be used in the hunt itself to surround and harpoon the whales.

Art. 44. The dimensions of the whaling sloops are fixed by law as follows: length, from 10 to 11.5 metres; width, from 1.8 to 1.95 metres.

Art. 45. The launches must have a weight of at least 4 tons and a speed of at least 8 knots.

Art. 51. In addition to such tools and equipment as are necessary for the hunt, all whaling boats must carry the following items on board:

an axe to cut the harpoon rope if this should be necessary; three flags, one white, one blue, one red; a box of biscuits; a container with fresh water; three Holmes luminous torches.

3. *Concerning the Conduct of the Hunt*

Art. 54. It is expressly forbidden to hunt whales with less than two boats.

Art. 55. It is forbidden to throw the harpoon when the boats are at such a distance from each other as not to be able to offer mutual assistance in the event of an accident.

Art. 56. In the event of an accident, all boats in the vicinity must assist those in difficulty, even if this means breaking off the hunt.

Art. 57. If a member of the crew should fall overboard during the hunt, the master of the boat involved will break off all hunting activity, cutting the harpoon rope if necessary, and will attend to the recovery of the man overboard to the exclusion of all else.

Art. 57a. If a boat captained by another master is present at the place where the accident occurs, this boat cannot refuse the necessary assistance.

Art. 57b. If the man overboard is the master, command will pass to the harpooneer, who must then follow the regulation described at Art. 57.

Art. 61. The direction of the hunt will be decided by the senior of the two masters, except where prior agreement to the contrary has been declared.

Art. 64.   In the event of dead or dying whales being found out at sea or along the coast, those who find them must immediately inform the maritime authorities who will have the responsibility of proceeding to verify the report and to remove any harpoons bearing registration numbers. In the event of such harpoons being found, the whales will be handed over to the legitimate owners of the harpoons. The finder of the whale will have the right to remuneration which will be paid under the terms of Art. 685 of the Commercial Code.

Art. 66.   It is expressly forbidden to throw loose harpoons (that is, not secured to the boat with a rope) at a whale, whatever the circumstances. Anyone who does so does not establish any right over the whale harpooned.

Art. 68.   No boat shall, without authorisation, cut the ropes of other boats, unless forced to do so to preserve their own safety.

Art. 69.   Harpoons, ropes, registration numbers, etc. found on a whale by other boats shall be returned to their rightful owners, nor does returning such items give any right to remuneration or indemnity.

Art. 70.   It is forbidden to harpoon or kill whales of the *Balaena* species, commonly known as *French whales*.

Art. 71.   It is forbidden to harpoon or kill female whales surprised while suckling their young, or young whales still at suckling age.

Art. 72.   In order to preserve the species and

better exploit hunting activities, it will be the responsibility of the Minister for the Sea to establish the sizes of the whales which may be caught and the periods of close season, to set quotas for the number of whales which may be hunted, and to introduce any other restrictive measures considered necessary.

Art. 73. The capture of whales for scientific purposes may be undertaken only after obtaining ministerial authorisation.

Art. 74. It is expressly forbidden to hunt whales for sport.

(*Regulations Governing the Hunting of Whales*, published in the 'Diário do Governo' 19.5.54 and still in force)

On the first Sunday in August the whalemen hold their annual festival in Horta. They line up their freshly-painted boats in Porto Pim bay, the bell briefly rings out two hoarse clangs, the priest arrives and blesses the boats. Then a procession forms and climbs up to the promontory dominating the bay where stands the chapel of Nossa Senhora da Guia. Behind the priest walk the women and children, with the whalemen bringing up the rear, each with his harpoon on his shoulder. They are very contrite and dressed in black. They all go into the chapel to hear Mass, leaving their harpoons standing against the wall outside, one next to the other, the way people elsewhere park their bicycles.

*

The harbour office is closed, but Senhor Chaves invites me in just the same. He is a distinguished, polite man with an open, slightly ironic smile and the blue eyes of some Flemish ancestor. There are hardly any left, he tells me, I don't think it'll be easy to find a boat. I ask if he means sperm-whales and he laughs, amused. No, whalemen, he specifies, they've all emigrated to America, every-body in the Azores emigrates to America, the Azores are deserted, haven't you noticed? Yes, of course I have, I say, I'm sorry. Why? he asks. It's an embarrassing question. Because I like the Azores, I reply without much logic. So you'll like them even more deserted, he objects. And then smiles as if to apologise for having been brusque. In any event, you see about getting yourself some life insurance, he concludes, otherwise I can't give you a permit. As for getting you on board, I'll sort that out, I'll speak to António José who may be going out tomorrow, it seems there's a herd on the way. But I can't promise you a permit for more than two days.

A Hunt

It's a herd of six or seven, Carlos Eugénio tells me, his satisfied smile showing off such a brilliant set of false teeth it occurs to me he might have carved them himself from whale ivory. Carlos Eugénio is seventy, agile and still youthful, and he is *mestre baleeiro*, which, literally translated, means 'master whaler', though in reality he is captain of this little crew and has absolute authority over every aspect of the hunt. The motor launch leading the expedition is his own, an old boat about ten metres long which he manoeuvres with deftness and nonchalance, and without any hurry either. In any event, he tells me, the whales are splashing about, they won't run away. The radio is on so as to keep in contact with the lookout based on a lighthouse on the island; a monotonous and it seems to me slightly ironic voice thus guides us on our way. 'A little to the right, Maria Manuela,' says the grating voice, 'you're going all over the place.' *Maria Manuela* is the name of the boat. Carlos Eugénio makes a gesture of annoyance, but still laughing, then he turns to the sailor who is riding with us, a lean, alert man, a boy almost, with constantly moving eyes and a dark complexion. We'll manage on our own, he decides and turns the radio off. The sailor climbs nimbly up the boat's only mast and perches on the crosspiece at the top, wrapping his legs around. He too points to the right. For a moment I think he's sighted them, but I don't know the whaleman's sign language. Carlos Eugénio explains that an open hand with the index finger pointing upward means 'whales in sight', and that wasn't the gesture our lookout made.

I turn to glance at the sloop we are towing. The whalemen are relaxed, laughing and talking together, though I can't make out what they're saying. They look as though they're out on a pleasure cruise. There are six of them and they're sitting on planks laid across the boat. The harpooneer is standing up though, and appears to be following our lookout's gestures with attention: he has a huge paunch and a thick beard, young, he can't be more than thirty. I've heard they call him Chá Preto, Black Tea, and that he works as a docker in the port in Horta. He belongs to the whaling cooperative in Faial and they tell me he's an exceptionally skilled harpooneer.

I don't notice the whale until we're barely three hundred metres away: a column of water rises against the blue as when some pipe springs a leak in the road of a big city. Carlos Eugénio has turned off the engine and only our momentum takes us drifting on towards that black shape lying like an enormous bowler hat on the water. In the sloop the whalemen are silently preparing for the attack: they are calm, quick, resolute, they know the motions they have to go through off by heart. They row with powerful well-spaced strokes and in a flash they are far away. They go round in a wide circle, approaching the whale from the front so as to avoid the tail, and because if they approached from the sides they would be in sight of its eyes. When they are a hundred metres off they draw their oars into the boat and raise a small triangular sail. Everybody adjusts sail and ropes: only the harpooneer is immobile on the point of the prow: standing, one leg bent forward, the harpoon lying in his hand as if he were measuring its weight. He concentrates, hanging on for the right moment, the moment when the boat will be near enough for him to strike a vital point, but far enough away not to be caught by a lash of the wounded whale's tail. Everything happens with amazing speed in just a few seconds. The boat makes a sudden turn while the harpoon is still curving through the air. The instrument of death isn't flung from above downwards, as I had expected, but upwards, like a javelin, and it is the sheer weight of the iron and the speed of the thing as it falls that transforms it into a deadly missile. When the enormous tail rises to whip first the air then the water, the sloop is already far away. The oarsmen are rowing again, furiously, and a strange play of ropes, which until now was going on underwater so that I hadn't seen it, suddenly becomes visible and I realise that our launch is connected to the harpoon too, while the whaling sloop has jettisoned its own rope. From a straw basket placed in a well in the middle of the launch, a thick rope begins to unwind, sizzling as it rushes through a fork on the bow; the young deckhand pours a bucket of water over it to cool it and prevent it snapping from the friction. Then the rope tightens and we set off with a jerk, a leap, following the wounded whale as it flees. Carlos Eugénio holds the helm and chews the stub of a cigarette; the sailor with the boyish face watches the sperm-whale's movements with a worried expression. In his hand he holds a small sharp axe ready to cut the rope if the whale should go down, since it would drag us with it under water. But the breathless rush doesn't last long. We've hardly gone a kilometre when the whale stops dead, apparently exhausted, and Carlos Eugénio has to put the launch into reverse to stop the momentum from taking us on top of the immobile animal. He struck well, he says with satisfaction, showing off his brilliant false teeth. As if in confirmation of his comment, the whale, whistling, raises his head right out of the water and breathes; and the jet that hisses up into the air is red with blood. A pool of vermilion spreads across the sea and the breeze carries a spray of red drops as far as our boat, spotting faces and clothes. The whaling sloop has drawn up against the launch: Chá Preto throws his tools up on deck and climbs up himself with an agility truly surprising for a man of his build. I gather that he wants to go on to the next stage of the attack, the lance, but the *mestre* seems not to agree. There follows some excited confabulation, which the sailor with the boyish face keeps out of. Then Chá Preto obviously gets his way; he stands on the prow and assumes his javelin-throwing stance, having swapped the harpoon for a weapon of the same size but with an extremely sharp head in an elongated heart shape, like a halberd. Carlos Eugénio moves forward with the engine on minimum, and the boat starts over to where the whale is breathing immobile in a pool of blood, restless tail spasmodically slapping the water. This time the deadly weapon is thrown downward; hurled on a slant, it penetrates the soft flesh as if it were butter. A dive: the great mass disappears, writhing underwater. Then the tail appears again, powerless, pitiful, like a black sail. And finally the huge head emerges and I hear the deathcry, a sharp wail, almost a whistle, shrill, agonising, unbearable.

The whale is dead and lies motionless on the water. The coagulated blood forms a bank that looks like coral. I hadn't realised the day was almost over and dusk surprises me. The whole crew are busy organising the towing. Working quickly, they punch a hole in the tail fin and thread through a rope with a stick to lock it. We are more than eighteen miles out to sea, Carlos Eugénio tells me; it will take all night to get back, the sperm-whale weighs around thirty tons and the launch will have to go very slowly. In a strange marine rope party led by the launch and with the whale bringing up the rear, we head towards the island of Pico and the factory of São Roque. In the middle is the sloop with the whalemen, and Carlos Eugénio suggests I join them so as to be able to get a little rest: under enormous strain, the launch's engine is making an infernal racket and sleep would be impossible. The two boats draw alongside each other and Carlos Eugénio leaves the launch with me, handing over the helm to the young sailor and two oarsmen who take our place. The whalemen set up a makeshift bed for me near the tiller; night has fallen and two oil lanterns have been lit on the sloop. The fishermen are exhausted, their faces strained and serious, tinted yellow in the light from the lanterns. They hoist the sail so as not to be a dead weight increasing the strain on the launch, then lie anyoldhow across the planks and fall into a deep sleep. Chá Preto sleeps on his back, paunch up, and snores loudly. Carlos Eugénio offers me a cigarette and talks to me about his two children who have emigrated to America and whom he hasn't seen for six years. They came back just once, he tells me, maybe they'll come again next summer. They'd like me to go to them, but I want to die here, at home. He smokes slowly and watches the sky, the stars. What about you though, why did you want to come with us today, he asks me, out of simple curiosity? I hesitate, thinking how to answer: I'd like to tell him the truth, but am held back by the fear that this might offend. I let a hand dangle in the water. If I stretched out my arm I could almost touch the enormous fin of the animal we're towing. Perhaps you're both a dying breed, I finally say softly, you people and the whales, I think that's why I came. Probably he's already asleep, he doesn't answer; though the coal of his cigarette still burns between his fingers. The sail slaps sombrely; motionless in sleep the bodies of the whalemen are small dark heaps and the sloop slides over the water like a ghost.

The Woman of Porto Pim
A Story

I sing every evening, because that's what I'm paid to do, but the songs you heard were *pesinhos* and *sapateiras* for the tourists and for those Americans over there laughing at the back. They'll get up and stagger off soon. My real songs are *chamaritas*, just four of them, because I don't have a big repertoire and then I'm getting on, and I smoke a lot, my voice is hoarse. I have to wear this *balandrau*, the traditional old Azores costume, because Americans like things to be picturesque, then they go back to Texas and say how they went to a tavern on a godforsaken island where there was an old man dressed in an ancient cloak singing his people's folksongs. They want the *viola de arame* which has this proud, melancholy sound, and I sing them sugary *modinhas*, with the same rhyme all the time, but it doesn't matter because they don't understand, and then as you can see, they're drinking gin and tonics. But what about you, though, what are you after, coming here every evening? You're curious and you're looking for something different, because this is the second time you've offered me a drink, you order *cheiro* wine as if you were one of us, you're a foreigner and you pretend to speak like us, but you don't drink much and then you don't say anything either, you wait for me to speak. You said you were a writer, and that maybe your job was something like mine. All books are stupid, there's never much truth in them, still I've read a lot over the last thirty years, I haven't had much else to do, Italian books too, all in translation of course. The one I liked most was called *Canaviais no vento*, by someone called Deledda, do you know it? And then you're young and you have an eye for the women, I saw the way you were looking at that beautiful woman with the long neck, you've been watching her all evening, I don't know if she's your girlfriend, she was looking at you too, and maybe you'll find it strange but all this has reawakened something in me, it must be because I've had too much to drink. I've always done things to excess in life, a road that leads to perdition, but if you're born like that you can't do anything about it.

In front of our house there was an *atafona*, that's what they're called on this island, a sort of wheel for drawing up water that turned round and round, they don't exist any more, I'm talking about years and years ago, before you were even born. If I think of it now, I can still hear it creaking, it's one of the childhood sounds that have stuck in my memory, my mother would send me with a pitcher to get some water and to make it less tiring I used to sing a lullaby as I pushed and sometimes I really would fall asleep. Beyond the water wheel there was a low whitewashed wall and then a sheer drop down to the sea. There were three of us children and I was the youngest. My father was a slow man, he used to weigh his words and gestures and his eyes were so clear they looked like water. His boat was called *Madrugada*, which was also my mother's maiden name. My father was a whaleman, like his father before him, but in the seasons when there were no whales, he used to fish for moray eels, and we went with him, and our mother too. People don't do it now, but when I was a child there was a ritual that was part of going fishing. You catch morays in the evening, with a waxing moon, and to call them there was a song which had no words: it was a song, a tune, that started low and languid, then turned shrill. I never heard a song so sorrowful, it sounded like it was coming from the bottom of the sea, or from lost souls in the night, a song as old as our islands. Nobody knows it any more, it's been lost, and maybe it's better that way, since there was a curse in it, or a destiny, like a spell. My father went out with the boat, it was dark, he moved the oars softly, dipping them in vertically so as not to make any noise, and the rest of us, my brothers and my mother, would sit on the rocks and start to sing. Sometimes the others would keep quiet, they wanted me to call the eels, because they said my voice was more melodious than anybody else's and the morays couldn't resist it. I don't believe my voice was any better than theirs: they wanted me to sing on my own because I was the youngest and people used to say that the eels liked clear voices. Perhaps it was just superstition and there was nothing in it, but that hardly matters.

Then we grew up and my mother died. My father became more taciturn and sometimes, at night, he would sit on the wall by the cliffs and look at the sea. By now we only went out after whales; we three boys were big and strong and Father gave us the harpoons and the lances, since he was getting too old. Then one day my brothers left. The second oldest went to America, he only told us the day he left, I went to the harbour to see him off, my father didn't come. The other went to be a truckdriver on the mainland, he was always laughing and he'd always loved the sound of engines; when the army man came to tell us about the accident I was at home alone and I told my father over supper.

We two still went out whaling. It was more difficult now, we had to take on casual labour for the day, because you can't go out with less than five, then my father would have liked me to get married, because a home without a woman isn't a real home. But I was twenty-five and I liked playing at love; every Sunday I'd go down to the harbour and get a new girlfriend. It was wartime in Europe and there were lots of people passing through the Azores. Every day a ship would moor here or on another island, and in Porto Pim you could hear all kinds of languages.

I met her one Sunday in the harbour. She was

wearing white, her shoulders were bare and she had a lace cap. She looked as though she'd climbed out of a painting, not from one of those ships full of people fleeing to the Americas. I looked at her a long time and she looked at me too. It's strange how love can find a way through to you. It got to me when I noticed two small wrinkles just forming round her eyes and I thought: she isn't that young. Maybe I thought like that because, being the boy I still was then, a mature woman seemed older to me than her real age. I only found out she wasn't much over thirty a lot later, when knowing her age would be of no use at all. I said good morning to her and asked if I could help her in any way. She pointed to the suitcase at her feet. Take it to the *Bote*, she said in my own language. The *Bote* is no place for a lady, I said. I'm not a lady, she answered, I'm the new owner.

Next Sunday I went down to town again. In those days the *Bote* was a strange kind of bar, not exactly a place for fishermen, and I'd only been there once before. I knew there were two private rooms at the back where rumour had it people gambled, and that the bar itself had a low ceiling, a large ornate mirror and tables made out of fig wood. The customers were all foreigners, they looked as though they were on holiday, while the truth was they spent all day spying on each other and pretending to come from countries they didn't really come from, and when they weren't spying they played cards. Faial was an incredible place in those days. Behind the bar was a Canadian called Denis, a short man with pointed sideburns who spoke Portuguese like someone from Cape Verde. I knew him because he came to the harbour on Saturdays to buy fish; you could eat at the *Bote* on Sunday evening. It was Denis who later taught me English.

I want to speak to the owner, I said. The owner doesn't come until after eight, he answered haughtily. I sat down at a table and ordered supper. She came in towards nine, there were other regulars around, she saw me and nodded vaguely, then sat in a corner with an old man with a white moustache. It was only then that I realised how beautiful she was, a beauty that made my temples burn. This was what had brought me there, but until then I hadn't really understood. And now, in the space of a moment, it all fell into place inside me so clearly it almost made me dizzy. I spent the evening staring at her, my temples resting on my fists, and when she went out I followed her at a distance. She walked with a light step, without turning; she didn't seem to be worried about being followed. She went under the gate in the big wall of Porto Pim and began to go down to the bay. On the other side of the bay, where the promontory ends, isolated among the rocks, between a cane thicket and a palm tree, there's a stone house. Maybe you've already noticed it. It's abandoned now and the windows are in poor shape, there's something sinister about it; some day the roof will fall in, if it hasn't already. She lived there, but in those days it was a white house with blue panels over the doors and windows. She went in and closed the door and the light went out. I sat on a rock and waited; halfway through the night a window lit up, she looked out and I looked at her. The nights are quiet in Porto Pim, you only need to whisper in the dark to be heard far away. Let me in, I begged her. She closed the shutter and turned off the light. The moon was coming up in a veil of red, a summer moon. I felt a great longing, the water lapped around me, everything was so intense and so unattainable, and I remembered when I was a child, how at night I used to call the eels from the rocks: then an idea came to me, I couldn't resist, and I began to sing that song. I sang it very softly, like a lament, or a supplication, with a hand held to my ear to guide my voice. A few moments later the door opened and I went into the dark of the house and found myself in her arms. I'm called Yeborath, was all she said.

Do you know what betrayal is? Betrayal, real betrayal, is when you feel so ashamed you wish you were somebody else. I wished I'd been somebody else when I went to say goodbye to my father and his eyes followed me about as I wrapped my harpoon in oilskin and hung it on a nail in the kitchen, then slung the viola he'd given me for my twentieth birthday over my shoulder. I've decided to change jobs, I told him quickly, I'm going to sing in a bar in Porto Pim, I'll come and see you Saturdays. But I didn't go that

Saturday, nor the Saturday after, and lying to myself I'd say I'd go and see him the next Saturday. So autumn came and the winter went, and I sang. I did other little jobs too, because sometimes customers would drink too much and to keep them on their feet or chase them off you needed a strong arm, which Denis didn't have. And then I listened to what the customers said while they pretended to be on holiday; it's easy to pick up people's secrets when you sing in a bar, and, as you see, it's easy to tell them too. She would wait for me in her house in Porto Pim and I didn't have to knock any more now. I asked her: who are you?, where are you from?, why don't we leave these absurd people pretending to play cards?, I want to be with you for ever. She laughed and left me to guess the reasons why she was living the way she was, and she said: wait just a little longer and we'll leave together, you have to trust me, I can't tell you any more. Then she'd stand naked at the window, looking at the moon, and say: sing me your eel song, but softly. And while I sang she'd ask me to make love to her, and I'd take her standing up, leaning against the windowsill, while she looked out into the night, as though waiting for something.

It happened on August 10th. It was São Lourenço and the sky was full of shooting stars, I counted thirteen of them walking home. I found the door locked and I knocked. Then I knocked again louder, because there was a light on. She opened and stood in the doorway, but I pushed

164

her aside. I'm going tomorrow, she said, the person I was waiting for has come back. She smiled, as if to thank me, and I don't know why but I thought she was thinking of my song. At the back of the room a figure moved. He was an old man and he was getting dressed. What's he want? he asked her in that language I now understood. He's drunk, she said; he was a whaler once but he gave up his harpoon for the viola, while you were away he worked as my servant. Send him away, said the man, without looking at me.

There was a pale light over Porto Pim. I went around the bay as if in one of those dreams where you suddenly find yourself at the other end of the landscape. I didn't think of anything, because I didn't want to think. My father's house was dark, since he went to bed early. But he wouldn't sleep, he'd lie still in the dark the way old people often do, as if that were a kind of sleep. I went in without lighting the lamp, but he heard me. You're back, he murmured. I went to the far wall and took my harpoon off the hook. I found my way in the moonlight. You can't go after whales at this time of night, he said from his bunk. It's an eel, I said. I don't know if he understood what I meant, but he didn't object, or get up. I think he lifted a hand to wave me goodbye, but maybe it was my imagination or the play of shadows in the half-dark. I never saw him again. He died long before I'd done my time. I've never seen my brother again either. Last year I got a photo of him, a fat man with white hair surrounded by a group of strangers who must be his sons and daughters-in-law, sitting on the veranda of a wooden house, and the colours are too bright, like in a postcard. He said if I wanted to go and live with him, there was work there for everybody and life was easy. That almost made me laugh. What could it mean, an easy life, when your life is already over?

And if you stay a bit longer and my voice doesn't give out, I'll sing you the song that decided the destiny of this life of mine. I haven't sung it for thirty years and maybe my voice isn't up to it. I don't know why I'm offering, I'll dedicate it to that woman with the long neck, and to the power a face has to surface again in another's, maybe that's what's touched a chord. And to you, young Italian, coming here every evening, I can see you're hungry for true stories to turn them into paper, so I'll make you a present of this story you've heard. You can even write down the name of the man who told it you, but not the name they know me by in this bar, which is a name for tourists passing through. Write that this is the true story of Lucas Eduino who killed the woman he'd thought was his, with a harpoon, in Porto Pim.

Oh, there was just one thing she hadn't lied to me about; I found out at the trial. She really was called Yeborath. If that's important at all.

Postscript
A Whale's View of Man

Always so feverish, and with those long limbs waving about. Not rounded at all, so they don't have the majesty of complete, rounded shapes sufficient unto themselves, but little moving heads where all their strange life seems to be concentrated. They arrive sliding across the sea, but not swimming, as if they were birds almost, and they bring death with frailty and graceful ferocity. They're silent for long periods, but then shout at each other with unexpected fury, a tangle of sounds that hardly vary and don't have the perfection of our basic cries: the call, the love cry, the death lament. And how pitiful their love-making must be: and bristly, brusque almost, immediate, without a soft covering of fat, made easy by their threadlike shape which excludes the heroic difficulties of union and the magnificent and tender efforts to achieve it.

They don't like water, they're afraid of it, and it's hard to understand why they bother with it. Like us they travel in herds, but they don't bring their females, one imagines they must be elsewhere, but always invisible. Sometimes they sing, but only for themselves, and their song isn't a call to others, but a sort of longing lament. They soon get tired and when evening falls they lie down on the little islands that take them about and perhaps fall asleep or watch the moon. They slide silently by and you realise they are sad.

Appendix

A Map, a Note, a few Books

A Map

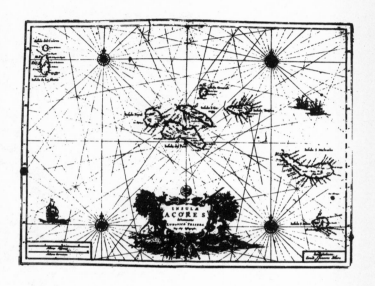

A Note

The Azores archipelago is situated in the middle of the Atlantic Ocean, about half-way between Europe and America, between latitudes 36°55′ and 39°44′N and longitudes 25° to 31°W. It is composed of nine islands: Santa Maria, São Miguel, Terceira, Graciosa, São Jorge, Pico, Faial, Flores and Corvo. The archipelago stretches across a distance of around 600 km from NW to SE. The name Azores is the result of an error on the part of the first Portuguese sailors; they mistook for sparrow-hawks (in Portuguese, *açores*) what in fact were the numerous kites which populate the islands.

Portuguese colonisation began in 1432 and went on for the whole of the fifteenth century, though at the same time the Azores also became the home of a large number of Flemish colonists, this as a result of marriages which linked the Portuguese throne with Flanders. The Flemish colonists left a considerable mark, not just on the physical features of the inhabitants, but also on the islands' popular music and folklore in general. The soil is volcanic in origin. The rocky coasts are often made up of sheets of extremely hard lava, while in flatter areas there are stretches of pulverised pumice stone. The physical characteristics of the landscape show very clear signs of volcanic and seismic activity. As well as a whole series of minor volcanic phenomena (smoke-holes, geysers, warm springs and mud swamps, etc.) there is an abundance of volcanic lakes which have taken over ancient craters, and the landscape is often broken by deep crevices scored out by the burning lava. The hinterland and the mountains have a savage and often gloomy beauty. The highest peak is Pico which is 2,345 metres high and located on the island of the same name. Innumerable volcanic eruptions have been recorded: the most terrifying earthquakes took place in 1522, 1538, 1591, 1630, 1755, 1810, 1862, 1884 and 1957. The effects of the 1978 earthquake, which hit the island of Terceira in particular, are clearly visible to any traveller stopping over in Angra. In the course of this incessant volcanic activity, the landscape of the Azores has been subjected to considerable change and countless little islands have surfaced and then disappeared. The most curious anecdote in this regard was told by an English sea-captain, Tillard. In 1810, on board his warship, the *Sabrina*, Tillard witnessed the birth of a little island on which he had two men land with an English flag, claiming possession of the territory for the English crown and baptising it Sabrina. But the day after, before lifting anchor, Captain Tillard was to find to his disappointment that the island of

Sabrina had disappeared and the sea was as flat and calm as ever.

The climate of the Azores is mild, with abundant but brief rainfalls and very hot summers. Nature is luxuriant and there are countless species of plants. Typically Mediterranean flora, in which cedars, vines, orange trees and pines dominate, flourishes alongside tropical vegetation which includes pineapple trees, banana trees, passion fruit and a huge variety of flowers. Birds and butterflies abound, but there are no reptiles. Whale hunting, using the traditional methods described in this book, is now practised only in Pico and Faial. In our century, the emigration of large numbers of people, mainly for economic reasons, has considerably depleted the archipelago's population. Corvo, Flores and Santa Maria are almost uninhabited.

A Few Books

ALBERT I, PRINCE OF MONACO, *La Carrière d'un Navigateur*, Monaco 1905 (with no publisher's name).

RAÚL BRANDÃO, *As Ilhas desconhecidas*, Bertrand, Rio–Paris 1926.

JOSEPH AND HENRY BULLAR, *A Winter in the Azores and a Summer at the Furnas*, John van Voorst, London 1841.

'Diário de Miss Nye', in *Insulana*, vol. XXIX–XXX, Ponta Delgada 1973–74.

J. MOUSINHO FIGUEIREDO, *Introdução ao estudo da indústria baleeira insular*, Astória, Lisbon 1945.

GASPAR FRUTUOSO, *Saudades da Terra*, 6 vols., Lisbon 1569–91 (a modern edition with updated orthography; Ponta Delgada 1963–64).

JULES MICHELET, *La Mer*, Hachette, Paris 1861.

ANTERO DE QUENTAL, *Sonetos*, Coimbra 1861 (and countless later editions).

Captain JOSHUA SLOCUM, *Sailing Alone around the World*, Rupert Hart-Davis, London 1940 (first edition 1900).

BERNARD VENABLES, *Baleia! The Whalers of the Azores*, The Bodley Head, London–Sydney–Toronto 1968.

The Flying Creatures of
Fra Angelico

The Flying Creatures of Fra Angelico

Note

Hypochondria, insomnia, restlessness and yearning are the lame muses of these brief pages. I would have liked to call them *Extravaganzas*, not so much for their style, as because many of them seem to wander about in a strange outside that has no inside, like drifting splinters, survivors of some whole that never was. Alien to any orbit, I have the impression they navigate in familiar spaces whose geometry nevertheless remains a mystery; let's say domestic thickets: the interstitial zones of our daily having to be, or bumps on the surface of existence.

Then some of these pages, as for example 'The Archives of Macao' and 'Past Composed: Three Letters', are eccentric even in their own terms, refugees from the idea that originated them. To the extent that they are fragments of novels and stories, they are no more than meagre conjectures, or spurious projections of desire. They have a larval nature: they present themselves like creatures under formalin, with the oversized eyes of organisms still in the foetal stage – questioning eyes. But questioning whom? What do they want? I don't know if they're really questioning anyone, nor if they want anything, but I feel it would be kinder to ask nothing of them, since I believe that asking questions is the prerogative of those beings Nature has not brought to completion: it is that which is clearly incomplete which has the right to ask questions. Still, I cannot deny that I love them, these sketchy compositions entrusted to a notebook which out of an unconscious sort of faithfulness I have carried around with me constantly these last few years. In them, in the form of quasi-stories, are the murmurings and mutterings that have accompanied and still accompany me: outbursts, moods, little ecstasies, real or presumed emotions, grudges and regrets.

So that rather than quasi-stories, perhaps I should say that these pages are no more than background noise in written form. Had I been a little more ruthless with myself, I would have called the collection *Buridan's Ass*. What stopped me from doing that, apart from a residual pride, which is often no more than a sublimated form of baseness, was the idea that although choice and completeness are not granted to the slothful wrapped up in their background noises, one is nevertheless still left with the chance of a few meagre words: so one may as well say them. A kind of awareness, this, not to be confused with noble stoicism, nor with resignation either.

A.T.

Some of these pieces have already been published in Italian or foreign reviews, though it would be difficult for me to supply an exact bibliography. All the same I would like to mention the original publications of two pieces which are linked to friends. Of the letters that make up 'Past Composed', published in *Il cavallo di Troia*, no. 4, 1983–84, the one from Dom Sebastião of Portugal to Francisco Goya was dedicated to José Sasportes, and I would like to renew that dedication. 'Message from the Half Dark' appeared in the catalogue (published by the Comune di Reggio Emilia, 1986) for a show of paintings by Davide Benati entitled *Terre d'ombre*. The piece is inspired by his paintings.

The Flying Creatures of
Fra Angelico

The first creature arrived on a Thursday
towards the end of June, at vespers, when all
the monks were in the chapel for service. Pri-
vately, Fra Giovanni of Fiesole still thought of
himself as Guidolino, the name he had left behind
in the world when he came to the cloister. He was
in the vegetable garden gathering onions, which
was his job, since in abandoning the world he
hadn't wanted to abandon the vocation of his
father, Pietro, who was a vegetable gardener, and
in the garden at San Marco he grew tomatoes,
courgettes and onions. The onions were the red
kind, with big heads, very sweet after you'd
soaked them for an hour, though they made you
cry a fair bit when you handled them. He was
putting them in his frock gathered to form an
apron, when he heard a voice calling: Guidolino.
He raised his eyes and saw the bird. He saw it
through onion tears filling his eyes and so stood
gazing at it for a few moments, for the shape was
magnified and distorted by his tears as though
through a bizarre lens; he blinked his eyes to dry
the lashes, then looked again.

It was a pinkish creature, soft looking, with

small yellowish arms like a plucked chicken's, bony, and two feet which again were very lean with bulbous joints and calloused toes, like a turkey's. The face was that of an aged baby, but smooth, with two big black eyes and a hoary down instead of hair; and he watched as its arms floundered wearily, as if unable to stop itself making this repetitive movement, miming a flight that was no longer possible. It had got caught up in the branches of the pear tree, which were spiky and warty and at this time of year laden with pears, so that at every one of the creature's movements, a few ripe pears would fall and land splat on the clods beneath. There it hung, in a very uncomfortable position, feet straddled over two branches which must be hurting its groin, torso sideways and neck twisted, since otherwise it would have been forced to look up in the air. From the creature's shoulderblades, like incredible triangular sails, rose two enormous wings which covered the entire foliage of the tree and which moved in the breeze together with the leaves. They were made of different coloured feathers, ochre, yellow, deep blue, and an emerald green the colour of a kingfisher, and every now and then they opened like a fan, almost touching the ground, then closed again, in a flash, disappearing behind each other.

Fra Giovanni dried his eyes with the back of his hand and said: 'Was it you called me?'

The bird shook its head and pointing a claw like an index finger towards him, wagged it.

'Me?' asked Fra Giovanni, amazed.

The bird nodded.

'It was me calling me?' repeated Fra Giovanni.

This time the creature closed his eyes and then opened them again, to indicate yes once again; or perhaps out of tiredness, it was hard to say: because he was tired, you could see it in his face, in the heavy dark hollows around his eyes, and Fra Giovanni noticed that his forehead was beaded with sweat, a lattice of droplets, though they weren't dripping down; they evaporated in the evening breeze and then formed again.

Fra Giovanni looked at him and felt sorry for him and muttered: 'You're overtired.' The creature looked back with his big moist eyes, then closed his eyelids and wriggled a few feathers in his wings: a yellow feather, a green one and two blue ones, the latter three times in rapid succession. Fra Giovanni understood and said, spelling it out as one learning a code: 'You've made a trip, it was too long.' And then he asked: 'Why do I understand what you say?' The creature opened his arms as far as his position allowed, as if to say, I haven't the faintest idea. So that Fra Giovanni concluded: 'Obviously I understand you because I understand you.' Then he said: 'Now I'll help you get down.'

Standing against a cherry tree at the bottom of the garden was a ladder. Fra Giovanni went and picked it up, and holding it horizontally on his shoulders with his head between two rungs, carried it over to the pear tree where he leaned it

184

in such a way that the top of the ladder was near the creature's feet. Before climbing up, he slipped off his frock because the skirts cramped his movements, and draped it over a sage bush near the well. As he climbed up the rungs he looked down at his legs, which were lean and white with hardly any hairs, and it occurred to him they looked like the bird creature's. And he smiled, since likenesses do make one smile. Then, as he climbed, he realised his private part had slipped out of the slit in his drawers and that the creature was staring at it with astonished eyes, shocked and frightened. Fra Giovanni did himself up, straightened his drawers and said: 'I'm sorry, it's something we humans have'; and for a moment he thought of Nerina, of a farmhouse near Siena many years before, a blonde girl and a straw rick. Then he said: 'Sometimes we manage to forget it, but it takes a lot of effort and a sense of the clouds above, because the flesh is heavy and forever pulling us earthwards.'

He grabbed the bird creature by the feet, freed him from the spikes of the pear tree, made sure that the down on his head didn't catch on the twigs, closed his wings, and then with the creature holding onto his back, brought him down to the ground.

The creature was droll: he couldn't walk. When he touched the ground he tottered, then fell on one side, and there he stayed, flailing about with his feet in the air like a sick chicken. Then he leaned on one arm and straightened his wings, rustling and whirling them like windmill sails, probably in an attempt to get up again. He didn't succeed, so Fra Giovanni gripped him under the armpits and pulled him up, and while he was holding the creature those frenetic feathers brushed back and forth across his face tickling him. Holding him almost suspended under these things that weren't quite armpits, he got him to walk, the way one does with a baby; and while they were walking, the creature's feathers opened and closed in a code Fra Giovanni understood, and asked him: 'What's this?' And he answered: 'This is earth, this is *the* earth.' And then, walking along the path through the garden, he explained that the earth was made of earth, and clods of soil, and that plants grew in the soil, such as tomatoes, courgettes, and onions for example.

When they reached the arches of the cloister, the creature stopped. He dug in his heels, stiffened and said he wouldn't go any further. Fra Giovanni put him down on the granite bench against the wall and told him to wait; and the creature stayed there, leaning up against the wall, staring dreamily at the sky.

'He doesn't want to be inside,' explained Fra Giovanni to the father superior, 'he's never been inside; he says he's afraid of being in an enclosed space, he can't conceive of space if it's not open, he doesn't know what geometry is.' And he explained that only he, Fra Giovanni, could see the creature, no one else. Well, because that's

186

how it was. The father superior, though only because he was a friend of Fra Giovanni's, might be able to hear the rustling of his wings, if he paid attention. And he asked: 'Can you hear?' And then he added that the creature was lost, had arrived from another dimension, wandering about; there'd been three of them and they'd got lost, a small band of creatures cast adrift, they had roamed aimlessly through skies, through secret dimensions, until this one had fallen into the pear tree. And he added that they would have to shelter him for the night under something that prevented him from floating up again, since when darkness came the creature suffered from the force of ascension, something he was subject to, and if there was nothing to hold him down he would float off up to wander about in the ether again like a splinter cast adrift, and they couldn't allow that to happen, they must offer the creature hospitality in the monastery, because in his way this creature was a pilgrim.

The father superior agreed and they tried to think what would be the best sort of shelter: something that was, yes, out in the open, but that would prevent any forced ascension. And so they took the garden netting that protected the vegetables from hedgehogs and moles; a net of hemp strings woven by the basket-weavers of Fiesole, who were very clever with wicker and yarn. They stretched the net over four poles which they set up at the bottom of the vegetable garden against the perimeter wall, so as to form a sort of open shed;

and on the clods of earth, which the bird creature found so strange, they placed a layer of dry straw, and laid the creature on top of it. After rearranging his little body a few times, he found the position he wanted on his side. He sank down with intense pleasure and, surrendering to the tiredness he must have dragged after him across the skies, immediately fell asleep. Upon which the monks likewise went to bed.

The other two creatures arrived the following morning at dawn while Fra Giovanni was going out to check the guest's chicken run and see if he had slept well. Against the pink glow of the dawning day he saw them approaching in a low, slanting flight, as if desperately trying, and failing, to maintain height, veering in fearful zigzags, so that at first he thought they were going to crash against the perimeter wall. But they cleared it by a hair's breadth and then, unexpectedly, regained height. One hovered in the air like a dragonfly, then landed with legs wide apart on the wall. He sat there a moment, astride the wall, as if undecided whether to fall down on this side or that, until at last he crashed down headfirst into the rosemary bushes in the flowerbed. The second creature meanwhile turned in two spiralling loops, an acrobat's pirouette almost, like a strange ball, because he was a rolypoly sort of being without a lower part to his body, just a chubby bust that ended in a greenish brushlike tail with thick, abundant plumage that must serve both as driving force and rudder. And like a ball he came down amongst the rows of lettuce, bouncing two or three times, so that what with his shape and greenish colour you would have thought he was a head of lettuce a bit bigger than the others off larking about thanks to some trick of nature.

For a moment Fra Giovanni was undecided as to whom he should go and help first. Then he chose the big dragonfly, because he seemed more in need, miserably caught as he was head down in the rosemary bushes, one leg sticking out and flailing about as if calling for help. When he went to pull him out he really did look like a big dragonfly, or at least that was the impression he gave; or rather, a large cricket, yes, that's what he looked like, so long and thin, and all gangly, with frail slender limbs you were afraid to touch in case they broke, almost translucent, pale green, like stems of unripe corn. And his chest was like a grasshopper's too, a wedge-shaped chest, pointed, without a scrap of flesh, just skin and bones: though there was the plumage, so sheer it almost seemed fur; golden; and the long shining hairs that sprouted from his skull were golden too, almost like hair, but not quite, and given the position of his body, head down, they were hiding his face.

Fearfully, Fra Giovanni stretched out an arm and pushed back the hair from its face: first he saw two big eyes, so pale they looked like water, gazing in amazement, then a thin, handsome face with white skin and red cheeks. A woman's face, because the features were feminine, albeit on a strange insectlike body. 'You look like Nerina,' Fra Giovanni said, 'a girl I once knew called Nerina.' And he began to free the creature from the rosemary needles, carefully, because he was afraid of breaking the thing; and because he was afraid he might snap her wings, which looked exactly like a dragonfly's, but large and stream-lined, transparent, bluish pink and gold with a very fine latticing, like a sail. He took the creature in his arms. She was fairly light, no heavier than a bundle of straw, and walking across the garden Fra Giovanni repeated what he had said the day before to the other creature; that this was the earth and that the earth was made of earth and of clods of soil and that in the soil grew plants, such as tomatoes, courgettes, and onions, for example.

He laid the bird creature in the cage next to the guest already there, and then hurried to fetch the other little creature, the rolypoly one that had wound up in the lettuces. Though it now turned out that he wasn't as rounded as he had seemed, his body having in the meantime as it were unrolled, to show that he had the shape of a loop, or of a figure of eight, though cut in half, since he was really no more than a bust terminating in a beauti-ful tail, and no bigger than a baby. Fra Giovanni picked him up and repeating his explanations about the earth and the clods took him to the cage, and when the others saw him coming they began to wriggle with excitement; Fra Giovanni put the little ball on the straw and watched with amaze-ment as the creatures exchanged affectionate looks, patted each other's feet and brushed each other's feathers, talking and even laughing with their wings at the joy of being reunited.

Meanwhile dawn had passed, it was daytime, the sun was already hot, and afraid that the heat might bother their strange skins, Fra Giovanni sheltered one side of the cage with twigs; then, after asking if they needed anything else and telling them if they did to please be sure to call him with their rustling noise, he went off to dig up the onions he needed to make the soup for lunch.

That night the dragonfly came to visit him. Fra Giovanni was asleep, he saw the creature sitting on the stool of his cell and had the impression of waking with a start, whereas in fact he was already awake. There was a full moon, and bright moonlight projected the square of the window onto the brick floor. Fra Giovanni caught an intense odour of basil, so strong it gave him a sort of heady feeling. He sat on his bed and said: 'Is it you smells of basil?' The creature laid one of her incredibly long fingers on her mouth as if to silence him and then came to him and embraced him. At which Fra Giovanni, confused by the night, by the smell of basil and by that pale face with the long hair, said: 'Nerina, it's you, I'm dreaming.' The creature smiled, and before leaving said with a rustle of wings: 'Tomorrow you must paint us, that's why we came.'

Fra Giovanni woke at dawn, as he always did, and straight after first prayers went out to the cage where the bird creatures were and chose the first model. A few days before, assisted by some of his brother monks, he had painted, in the twenty-third cell in the monastery, the crucifixion of Christ. He had asked his helpers to paint the background *verdaccio*, a mixture of ochre, black and vermilion, since he wanted this to be the colour of Mary's desperation as she points, petrified, at her crucified son. But now that he had this little round creature here, tail elusive as a flame, he thought that to lighten the virgin's grief and have her understand how her son's suffering was God's will, he would paint some divine beings who, as instruments of the heavenly plan, consented to bang the nails into Christ's hands and feet. He thus took the creature into the cell, set him down on a stool, on his stomach so that he looked as though he were in flight, and painted him like that at the corners of the cross, placing a hammer in his right hand to drive in the nails: and the monks who had frescoed the cell with him looked on in astonishment as with incredible rapidity his brush conjured up this strange creature from the shadows of the crucifixion, and with one voice they said: 'Oh!'

So the week passed with Fra Giovanni painting so much he even forgot to eat. He added another figure to an already completed fresco, the one in cell thirty-four, where he had already painted Christ praying in the Garden. The painting looked finished, as if there were no more space to fill; but he found a little corner above the trees to the right and there he painted the dragonfly with Nerina's face and the translucent golden wings. And in her hand he placed a chalice, so that she could offer it to Christ.

Then, last of all, he painted the bird creature who had arrived first. He chose the wall in the corridor on the first floor, because he wanted a wide wall that could be seen from a good distance. First he painted a portico, with Corinthian columns and capitals, and then a glimpse of garden ending in a palisade. Finally he arranged the creature in a genuflecting pose, leaning him against a bench to prevent him from falling over; he had him cross his hands on his breast in a gesture of reverence and said to him: 'I'll cover you with a pink tunic, because your body is too ugly. I'll draw the Virgin tomorrow. You hang on this afternoon and then you can all go. I'm doing an Annunciation.'

By evening he had finished. Night was falling and he felt a little tired, and melancholy too, that melancholy that comes when something is finished and there is nothing left to do and the moment has passed. He went to the cage and found it empty. Just four or five feathers had got caught in the net and were twitching in the fresh wind coming down from the Fiesole hills. Fra Giovanni thought he could smell an intense odour of basil, but there was no basil in the garden. There were the onions that had been waiting to be picked for a week now and perhaps were already going off, soon they wouldn't be good enough for making soup any more. So he set off to pick them before they went rotten.

Past Composed: Three Letters

I

Letter from Dom Sebastião de Avis,* King of Portugal, to Francisco Goya, painter

In this shadow world I inhabit, where the future is already present, I have heard tell that your hands are unrivalled in the depiction of carnage and caprice. Your home is Aragon, a land dear to me for its solitude, for the geometry of its roads, for the quiet green of its courtyards hidden behind bellied gratings.

*Dom Sebastião de Avis (1554–78) was the last Portuguese king of the house of Avis. He came to the throne while still a child, was raised in an atmosphere of mysticism, and came to believe he had been chosen by God to accomplish great deeds. Nursing his dream to subject all Barbary to his rule and extend his kingdom as far as the revered Palestine, he put together a huge army, made up mostly of adventurers and beggars, and set off on a crusade that was to spell disaster for Portugal. In August 1578, exhausted by the heat and a forced march across the desert, the Portuguese army was destroyed by the light cavalry of the Moors near Alcácer-Quibir. Sebastião had left no direct descendants; with his death, Portugal was subjected to foreign domination for the first and only time in its history. Annexed to the crown of Spain by Philip II, it regained its independence in 1640 after a national rebellion.

There are dark chapels with sorrowful portraits, relics, braids of hair in glass cases, phials
of real tears and real blood; and small arenas
where lithe men stalk the captive beast with the
agile steps of dancers. Your land embodies some
quintessential virtue of our peninsula in its lines,
its faith, its fury. From these I shall choose some
images for the symbol which, as heraldic emblem
of a unique nation, you shall inscribe in the
borders of the painting I hereby commission from
you.

So then: On the right you shall paint the Sacred
Heart of Our Lord. It will be dripping and bound
in thorns, as in the images sold by pedlars and
blind men in the squares outside our churches.
But it must faithfully reproduce man's real ana-
tomy, since to suffer on the cross Our Lord
became a man, and His heart burst like a human
heart and was pierced like any muscle of flesh.
You shall paint it like that, muscular, throbbing,
swollen with blood and pain, showing the lace-
work of the veins, the severed arteries, and the
intricate latticework of the surrounding mem-
brane open like a curtain and folded back like
the peel of a fruit. It would be well to thrust the
spear that transfixed it into the heart, the blade
being shaped like a hook so as to tear open the
wound from which His blood pours freely down.

On the opposite side of the painting, halfway
up, and therefore level with the horizon, you
shall paint a small bull. Paint him lying on his
haunches, his front legs stretched out before him,

like a pet dog; and his horns must be diabolical and his countenance evil. In the physiognomy of this monster you shall demonstrate that flair for the fantastical wherein you excel. Thus a sneer shall twist the animal's muzzle, but the eyes must be innocent, almost childlike. The weather shall be misty; the hour, dusk. The merciful, soft shadow of evening will already be falling, veiling the scene. The ground will be littered with corpses, thousands of corpses, thick as flies. You shall depict them as only you know how, incongruous and innocent as the dead always are. And beside the corpses, and in their arms, you shall paint the viols and guitars they took with them to their deaths.

In the middle of the painting, high up, amidst clouds and sky, you shall paint a ship. Not a ship drawn from life, but something from a dream, an apparition, a chimera. For this must be all the ships that took my people across foreign seas to distant coasts or down to the bottomless depths of the ocean, and again all the dreams my people dreamt looking out from the cliffs where my country runs to meet the sea, the monsters they conjured up in their imaginations, and the fables, the fish, the dazzling birds, the mourning and the mirages. And at the same time it shall also be my own dreams, the dreams I inherited from ancestors and my own silent folly. The figurehead of this ship shall have a human form and you must paint its features so that they seem alive and distantly recall my own. A smile may hover over

them, but it must be faint, or vaguely mysterious:
the incurable, subtle nostalgia of one who knows
that all is vanity and that the winds which swell
the sails of dreams are nothing but air, air, air.

II

Letter from Mademoiselle Lenormand,*
fortune-teller, to Dolores Ibarruri, revolutionary

My cards portray ladies in sumptuous brocades,
coffers, castles, and graceful dancing skeletons,
not at all macabre and well-suited to predict
triumph and death to delicate princes and hot-
tempered emperors. I do not know why they are
asking me to read the story of your life, which has
not yet begun and which, given the many years
that separate it from this present time, I discern
only through broad, perhaps deceptive rents in
the veil. Perhaps it is because, despite your
humble birth, something in your destiny does
partake of the nature of monarchs and lords: that
profound sadness, like a fatal disease, of those
who have the power to decide the fate of others,
to dispose of men and women and to move, albeit
for a noble end, poor human lives across the
chessboard of destiny.

*Mademoiselle Lenormand was Napoleon's fortune-teller
and one of the most celebrated French clairvoyants of her
time.

You will be born in the heart of Spain, in a village whose name is unclear to me, veiled in black gritty dust. Your father will plunge into the dark every morning at dawn, reappearing in the dead of night, heavy with filth and fatigue, to sleep like a rock in a bed near your own. Encased in the shell of her black dress, your mother will be silent and pious, terrified of what the future may bring. They will call you Dolores, out of Christian reverence, not realising that it foreshadows the nature of your life.

Your childhood will be utterly empty, I can see that clearly. You will not even wish for a doll, since never having seen one you will be unable to imagine such a thing, but simply cherish a vague longing for some kind of human shape onto which to transfer your childhood terrors. Your mother, poor ignorant woman, doesn't know how to stitch together a doll, doesn't realise that children need games, since what they most need is food.

You will grow up with the righteous anger of the poor when they refuse to become resigned. You will speak to those the powerful think of as dirt and you will teach them not to become like your mother. You will kindle hope in them, and they will follow you. For how could the poor live without hope?

You will suffer the threats of judges, the beatings of the police, the coarseness of prison guards, the contempt of servants. But you will be beautiful, impetuous, fearless, blazing with scorn. They will call you 'La Pasionaria', because of the fire that burns in your heart.

Then I see war. You will organise your people: on your side you will have the lowly and those who believe that men can be redeemed, and that will be your banner. You will even fight ideals similar to your own, because you consider them less perfect. And meanwhile the real enemy will defeat you. You will experience flight, exile, one hiding place after another. You will live on silence and scraps of bread, and at sunset the long straight roads will point to the horizons of lands as alien to you as those you are fleeing. Haylofts and stables, ditches, unknown comrades, people's compassion – these will be your shelter.

You are dark-haired and dark-eyed, a woman of the South, accustomed to blond, sun-drenched landscapes dotted here and there with the white of Don Quixote's windmills. You will find refuge in the great plains of the East, where the deep winter cold cracks both earth and hearts. Your voice has a resonant Latin cadence with syllables ringing like the clapping of hands: you speak a language made for guitars, for festivals in orange groves, for challenges in the arena where brave, stupid men grapple with the beast. The tongue of the steppes will sound barbaric, but you will have to use it and forget your own. They will give you a medal; every year, in early May, you will sit on a platform beside taciturn men, likewise wearing medals, to watch soldiers in dress uniform file by below, while the wind spreads the red of the flags and the thundering notes of martial anthems played by machines. You will be a veteran with a flat – reward in bricks and mortar for your heroism.

War again. Some are destined to witness death and destruction: you are one of them. In a city that will come to be called Stalingrad, death will snatch away the son you bore, the one real solace of your existence. My God, how quickly the years fly by in my cards, in your regrets! Only yesterday he was a child, and now he's a soldier already, and dead. You will be the heroic mother of a hero; your breast will bear another medal. The war is over now. Moscow. I see stealthy footsteps crossing the snow; a pure white blanket tries in vain to blur my cards; I sense the funereal gloom that pervades the city. At the carriage-stops everyone stares at the ground to avoid meeting their neighbours' eyes.

And you too will be cautious, coming home of an evening, for this is a time of suspicion. At night you will wake with a start, soaked in sweat, unsure even of your own loyalty, since the worst heresy is to believe oneself in possession of the truth, and pride has brought down many. You will search your conscience long and hard. And where have your old comrades gone meanwhile? Vanished, all of them. You will toss and turn in your bed, the sheets will be thorns. Outside it is bitterly cold; how can the pillow burn so fiercely?

'All traitors?'

'Every one.'

'Even Francisco who laughed like a child and sang the *romancero*?'

'Even Francisco.'

'Even El Campesino who wept with you over your dead?'

Yes, even El Campesino – he's cleaning Moscow's toilets now. And your short sleep will already be over. You are sitting on your bed, eyes fixed on the opposite wall, staring into the shadows (you always leave a night-light on – you can't bear the darkness). But what else can you do? South America is too far away, and besides, they won't let La Pasionaria leave the friendly confines of Russia.

So you decide you had better cling to your ideals, make of them an even stronger faith, stronger and stronger and stronger still. And then after all, time is passing. Slowly, very slowly, but all things do pass. Men pass away, and suffering, and disasters. You too will almost be ready to pass away, and that will be a source of subtle, secret comfort. The meagre bun of your hair will turn white with age and grief. Your face will be dry, ascetic, with two deep hollows. Then your king will die too. You will take your place beside the coffin in the middle of the square, you will stay there day and night, always wholly yourself, silent, inflexible, your eyes always open, while a huge crowd files mutely by the embalmed corpse. Priestly, statuesque, carved in flint – 'That is La Pasionaria,' people will think when they see you, and here and there a father will point you out to his son. While all the time, to stop yourself giving way to the panic and longing which have carved out tunnels in your soul, the hands in your lap will be twisting and twisting your handkerchief, until you tie it into a knot (how strange, why are you stroking that little round wad?). And in your mind you see a room that time has borne away, a bare iron bed and a tiny Dolores, frightened and sick, with feverish eyes, calling plaintively, '*Mamaita, el jugete. Mamaita, por favor, el jugete.*' And your mother gets up from her chair and makes you something like a doll, knotting together the corners of her brown handkerchief.

Many more years await you, but they will all be the same. Dolores Ibarruri, when you look in your mirror what you see will be the image of La Pasionaria, it will never change.

Then one day, perhaps, you will read my letter. Or you won't read it, but this will not have the slightest importance, because you will be old, and everything will already have been. Because if life could go back and be different from what has been, it would annihilate time and the succession of cause and effect that is life itself, and that would be absurd. And my cards, Dolores, cannot change what, since it has to be, has already been.

III

Letter from Calypso, a nymph,
to Odysseus, King of Ithaca

Purple and swollen like secret flesh are the petals of Ogygia's flowers; brief showers, soft and warm, feed the bright green of her woods; no winter troubles the waters of her streams.

Barely the blink of an eye has passed since your departure, which seems so remote to you, and your voice calling farewell to me from the sea still wounds my divine hearing in this insuperable now. Every day I watch the sun's chariot race across the sky and I follow its course towards your west; I look at my white, unchanging hands; I trace a mark in the sand with a twig, as if adding a number to some futile reckoning, and then I erase it. And I have traced and erased many thousands of marks: the gesture is the same, the sand is the same, I am the same. And everything else.

But you live in change. Your hands have become bony, with protruding knuckles; the firm blue veins that ran across them have come to resemble the knotty rigging of your ship, and if a child plays with them, the blue ropes slither away under the skin and the child laughs and measures the smallness of his own small hand against your palm. Then you lift him down from your knees and set him on the ground, because a memory of long ago has caught up with you and a shadow crosses your face. But he runs around you, shouting happily, and at once you pick him up again and sit him on the table in front of you. Something deep, something that can't be put into words takes place, and intuitively you grasp the substance of time in the transmission of the flesh.

But what is the substance of time, and how can it come into being, if everything is fixed, unchanging, one? At night I gaze at the spaces between the stars, I see the boundless void, and what overwhelms you humans and sweeps you away is only one fixed moment here, without beginning or end.

Oh, Odysseus, to be able to escape this eternal green! To be able to follow the leaves as they yellow and fall, to live the moment with them! To discover myself mortal!

I envy your old age and I long for it; that is the form my love for you takes. And I dream of another Calypso, old and grey and feeble, and I dream of feeling my strength dwindling, of sensing every day that I am a little closer to the Great Circle where everything returns and revolves, of scattering the atoms that make up this woman's body I call Calypso. And yet here I remain, staring at the sea as it ebbs and flows, feeling no more than its reflection, suffering this weariness of being that devours me and will never be appeased – and the empty terror of eternity.

The Passion of Dom Pedro

A man, a woman, passion and unreasoned revenge are the characters of this story. The white pebbled banks of the River Mondego where it flows beneath Coimbra provide the setting. Time, which as a concept is essential to the tale, is of little importance in chronological terms: for the record, however, I will say that we are halfway through the fourteenth century.

The opening scenario smacks of the banal. Marriages of convenience dictated by diplomacy and the need to establish alliances were banal in those times. Likewise banal was the young prince Dom Pedro sitting in his palace awaiting the arrival of his betrothed, a noble woman from nearby Spain. And in banal fashion, as custom and tradition would have it, the nuptial delegation arrived: the future bride, her guards, her maids of honour. I would even venture to say that it was banal that the young prince should fall in love with one of the maids in waiting, the tender Inês de Castro who in the manner of the time contemporary chroniclers and poets described as being slender of neck and rosy of cheek. Banal because, if it was common for a monarch to marry not a woman but a reason of state, it was equally common for him to satisfy his desires as a man with a woman to whom he was attracted for motives other than those of political convenience.

But the young Dom Pedro was a stubborn and determined monogamist; that is the first element in our story which is not banal. Fired by an exclusive and indivisible love for the tender Inês, Dom Pedro infringed the subtle canons of concealment and the prudent heedings of diplomacy. The marriage had been imposed on him for strictly dynastic reasons, and from a strictly dynastic point of view he did abide by it: but having produced the heir his father wanted of him, he moved together with Inês into a castle on the Mondego, and without marrying made her his real spouse: which is the second element in our story which is not banal. At this point the cold violence of reason enters the scene in the shape of a pitiless executioner. The old king was a wise and prudent man and in loving his son loved not so much the son himself as the king his son would become. He gathered together his councillors of the realm and they suggested a remedy they felt would settle the problem once and for all: the elimination of this obstacle to the good of the state. While the prince was away, Dona Inês was put to death by the sword, as a chronicler tells us, in her house in Coimbra.

Years went by. The legitimate queen had died some time ago. Then one day the old father died too and Dom Pedro was king. Now his vendetta could begin. At first it was a cruel and foul vendetta, but one which nevertheless still partook of human logic. With prodigious patience and the meticulousness of a solicitor's clerk, he had his police trace all of his father's old councillors. Some, already old and retired, were living quiet lives away from the public eye; others were difficult to find: plausible fears had prompted them to leave Portugal and offer their services to other monarchs. Dom Pedro waited for them one by one in the courtyard of his palace. He was haunted by insomnia. Some nights he would get up and break the unbearable silence of his rooms by having the servants light all the torches and by calling the trumpeters and ordering them to play. The chronicler of the period who recorded these events is prodigal with his details: he describes the bare, austere courtyard, the echoing of horses' hooves on stone, the rattle of chains, the shouts of the guards announcing the capture of another wanted man. He describes too how Dom Pedro waited patiently, standing motionless at a window from which he could look down on the courtyard and the road whence his victims must come. He was a tall man, very thin, with an ascetic face and long pointed beard, like a physician or a priest, and he always wore the same cloak over the same jerkin. Our meticulous chronicler even gives us the words, or rather supplications the prisoners addressed to their torturer, and to which he never replied: for the king would do nothing more than supply details of a technical nature indicating what he felt would be the most fitting way to put an end to a victim's life. Dom Pedro was not without reserves of irony: for a prisoner called Coelho, which in Portuguese means 'rabbit', he chose death over a gridiron. But in every case, and sometimes while they were still alive, he would have the victim's chest ripped open and the heart removed and brought to him on a copper tray. He would take the still warm organ in his hands and toss it to a pack of greedy dogs waiting below on the terrace.

But his bloody vendetta, which horrified our good chronicler, did not prove an effective placebo for Dom Pedro. His resentment at having been crushed by events now irremediable was not to be satisfied by the cardiac muscle of a few courtiers: in the stony loneliness of his palace he meditated a more subtle revenge which concerned not the pragmatic or human planes, but that of time itself and of the concatenation of events which make up our lives – events which in this case were already past. He decided to retrieve the irretrievable.

It was a hot Coimbra summer and lavender and broom were flourishing along the pebbly banks of the river. The washerwomen beat their laundry in the lazy trickle that snaked between the stones; and they sang. Dom Pedro realised that everything – his subjects, that river, the flowers, the songs, his very being there as king – would have been the same even if everything had been different and nothing had happened; and that the tremendous plausibility of existence, inexorable as reality always is, was more solid than his ferocity, could not be wiped out by any vendetta of his. What exactly did the king think as he looked out of his window across the white plains of Portugal? What kind of sorrow was it that haunted him? The nostalgia for what has been may be heart-rending; but nostalgia for what we would have liked to happen, for what might have been and never was, must be intolerable. Probably it was this nostalgia that was crushing Dom Pedro. Every night, in his incurable insomnia, he would look up at the stars: and perhaps it was the interstellar distances, those spaces immeasurable in terms of human time which gave him the idea. Perhaps that subtle irony which he nursed in his heart along with the nostalgia for what hadn't been also played its part. In any event he thought up a brilliant plan.

As we have seen, Dom Pedro was a man of few words and strong character: the following morning a terse notice announced a great feast for the people throughout the kingdom, the coronation of a queen and a solemn nuptial procession in the midst of an exultant crowd all the way from Coimbra to Alcobaça. Dona Inês was exhumed from her tomb. The chronicler does not tell us whether she was already a bare skeleton or in what state of decomposition otherwise. She was dressed in white, crowned and placed on an open royal coach to the right of the king. The couple were pulled by a pair of white horses with big coloured plumes. Silver harness bells on the horses' heads jingled brightly at every step. The crowd, as ordered, walked either side of the nuptial procession, marrying the reverence of subjects with their repugnance. I am inclined to believe that Dom Pedro, careless of appearances, from which anyway he was protected by the powers of a considerable imagination, was convinced he was riding, not with the corpse of his old lover, but with the real Inês before her death. One could maintain that he was essentially mad, but that would be an evident simplification.

It is eighty kilometres from Coimbra to Alcobaça. Dom Pedro came back alone and incognito from his imaginary honeymoon. Awaiting Dona Inês in the abbey at Alcobaça was a stone tomb the king had had sculpted by a famous artist. Opposite Inês's sarcophagus, on the lid of which she was shown in all her youthful beauty, and arranged *pied à pied* so that come the day of judgement their residents would find themselves face to face, was a similar sarcophagus bearing the image of the king.

Dom Pedro was to wait many years before taking his place in the tomb he had prepared for himself. He passed this time fulfilling his kingly duties: he minted gold and silver coins, brought peace to his kingdom, chose a woman to brighten up his rooms; he was an exemplary father, a discreet and courteous friend, a fair administrator of justice. He even experienced happiness and gave parties. But these would seem to be irrelevant details. In all likelihood those years had a different rhythm for him than the rhythm of other men. They were all the same, and perhaps passed in a flash, as if they had already been.

Message from the Shadows

In these latitudes night falls suddenly, hard upon a fleeting dusk that lasts but an instant, then the dark. I must live only in that brief space of time, the rest of the day I don't exist. Or rather, I am here, but it's as if I weren't, because I'm elsewhere, there where I left you, yes, and then everywhere, in every place on earth, on the waters, in the wind that swells the sails of ships, in the travellers who cross the plain, in the city squares with their merchants and their voices and the anonymous flow of the crowd. It's difficult to say what my shadow world is made of and what it means. It's like a dream you know you are dreaming, that's where its truth lies: in its being real beyond the real. Its structure is that of the iris, or rather of fleeting gradations, already gone while still there, like time in our lives. I have been granted the chance to go back over it, that time no longer mine which once was ours; it runs swiftly inside my eyes; so fast that I make out places and landscapes where we lived together, moments we shared, even our conversations of long ago, do you remember? We would talk about parks in Madrid, about a fisherman's house where we would have liked to live, about windmills and the rocky cliffs falling sheer into the sea one winter night when we ate bread soup, and of the chapel with the fishermen's votive offerings: madonnas with the faces of local women and castaways like puppets who save themselves from the waves by holding onto a beam of sunlight pouring down from the heavens. But all this flickers by inside my eyes and although I can decipher it and do so with minute exactness, it's so fast in its inexorable passage that it becomes just a colour: the mauve of morning in the highlands, the saffron of the fields, the indigo of a September night with the moon hung on the tree in the clearing outside the old house, the strong smell of the earth and your left breast that I loved more than the right, and life was there, calmed and measured out by the cricket who lived nearby, and that was the best night of all nights, liquid as the pulp of an apricot.

In the time of this infinitesimal infinite, which is the space between my now and our then, I wave you goodbye and I whistle 'Yesterday', and 'Guaglione'. I have laid my pullover on the seat next to mine, the way I used to when we went to the cinema and I waited for you to come back with the peanuts.

'The phrase that follows this is false: the phrase that precedes this is true'

Madras, 12 January 1985

Dear Mr Tabucchi,

Three years have gone by since we met at the Theosophical Society in Madras. I will admit that the place was hardly the most propitious in which to strike up an acquaintance. We barely had time for a brief conversation, you told me you were looking for someone and writing a little diary about India. You seemed to be very curious about onomastics; I remember you liking my name and asking my permission to use it, albeit disguised, in the book you were writing. I suspect that what interested you was not so much myself as two other things: my distant Portuguese origins and the fact that I knew the works of Fernando Pessoa. Perhaps our conversation was somewhat eccentric: in fact its departure point was two adverbs used frequently in the West (*practically* and *actually*), from which we attempted to arrive at the mental states which preside over such adverbs. All of which led us, with a certain logic, to talk about pragmatism and transcendence, shifting the conversation, perhaps inevitably, to the plane of our respective religious beliefs. I remember your professing yourself to be, it seemed to me with a little embarrassment, an agnostic, and when I asked you to imagine how you might one day be reincarnated, you answered that if ever this were to happen you would doubtless return as a lame chicken. At first I thought you were Irish, perhaps because the Irish, more than the English, have their own special way of approaching the question of religion. I must say in all honesty that you made me suspicious. Usually Europeans who come to India can be divided into two groups: those who believe they have discovered transcendence and those who profess the most radical secularism. My impression was that you were mocking both attitudes, and in the end I didn't like that. We parted with a certain coldness. When you left I was sure your book, if you ever wrote it, would be one of those intolerable western accounts which mix up folklore and misery in an incomprehensible India.

I admit I was wrong. Reading your *Indian Nocturne* prompted a number of considerations which led me to write you this letter. First of all I would like to say that if the theosopher in Chapter Six is in part a portrayal of myself, then it is a clever and even amusing portrait, albeit characterised by a severity I don't believe I

deserve, but which I find plausible in the way you
see me. But these are not, of course, the considerations that prompted me to write to you. Instead I
would like to begin with a Hindu phrase which
translated into your language goes more or less
like this: the man who thinks he knows his (or his
own?) life, in fact knows his (or his own?) death.

I have no doubt that *Indian Nocturne* is about
appearances, and hence about death. The whole
book is about death, especially the parts where it
talks about photography, about the image, about
the impossibility of finding what has been lost:
time, people, one's own image, history (as understood by western culture at least since Hegel, one
of the most doltish philosophers, I think, that
your culture has produced). But these parts of
the book are also an initiation, of which some
chapters form secret and mysterious steps. Every
initiation is mysterious, there's no need to invoke
Hindu philosophy here because western religions
believe in this mystery too (the Gospel). Faith is
mysterious and in its own way a form of initiation. But I'm sure the most aware of western
artists do sense this mystery as we do. And in this
regard permit me to quote a statement by the
composer Emmanuel Nunes, whom I had occasion to hear recently in Europe: 'Sur cette route
infinie, qui les unit, furent bâties deux cités: la
Musique et la Poésie. La première est née, en
partie, de cet élan voyageur qui attire le Son vers
le Verbe, de ce désir vital de sortir de soi-même,
de la fascination de l'Autre, de l'aventure qui

consiste à vouloir prendre possession d'un sens qui n'est pas le sien. La seconde jaillit de cette montée ou descente du Verbe vers sa propre origine, de ce besoin non moins vital de revisiter le lieu d'effroi où l'on passe du non-être à l'être.'

But I would like to turn to the end of your book, the last chapter. During my most recent trip to Europe, after buying your book, I looked up a few newspapers for the simple curiosity of seeing what the literary critics thought about the end. I could not, of course, be exhaustive, but the few reviews I was able to read confirmed what I thought. It was evident that western criticism could not interpret your book in anything but a western manner. And that means through the tradition of the 'double', Otto Rank, Conrad's *The Secret Sharer*, psychoanalysis, the literary 'game' and other such cultural categories charac-teristic of the West. It could hardly be otherwise. But I suspect that you wanted to say something different; and I also suspect that that evening in Madras when you confessed to knowing nothing about Hindu philosophy, you were — why, I don't know — lying (telling lies). As it is, I think you are familiar with oriental gnosticism and with those western thinkers who have followed the path of gnosticism. You are familiar with the Mandala, I'm sure, and have simply transferred it into your culture. In India the preferred symbol of whole-ness is usually the Mandala (from the Latin *mundus*, in Sanskrit 'globe', or 'ring'), and then the zero sign, and the mirror. The zero, which the

West discovered in the fourth century after Christ, served in India as a symbol of Brahma and of Nirvana, matrix of everything and of nothing, light and dark; it was also an equivalent of the 'as if' of duality as described in the Upanishads. But let us take what for westerners is a more comprehensible symbol: the mirror. Let us pick up a mirror and look at it. It gives us an identical reflection of ourselves, but inverting left and right. What is on the right is transposed to the left and vice versa with the result that the person looking at us is ourselves, but not the same self that another sees. In giving us our image inverted on the back–front axis, the mirror produces an effect that may even conceal a sort of sorcery: it looks at us from outside, but it is as if it were prying inside us; the sight of ourselves does not leave us indifferent, it intrigues and disturbs us as that of no other: the Taoist philosophers call it *the gaze returned*.

Allow me a logical leap which you perhaps will understand. We are looking at the gnosis of the Upanishads and the dialogues between Misargatta Maharaj and his disciples. Knowing the Self means discovering in ourselves that which is already ours, and discovering furthermore that there is no real difference between being in me and the universal wholeness. Buddhist gnosis goes a step further, beyond return: it nullifies the Self as well. Behind the last mask, the Self turns out to be absent.

I am reaching the conclusion of what, I appreciate, is an overly long letter, and probably an impertinence that our relationship hardly justifies. You will forgive me a last intrusion into your privacy, justified in part by the confession you made me that evening in Madras vis-à-vis your likely reincarnation, a confession I haven't the audacity to consider a mere whim. Even Hindu thinking, despite believing that the way of Karma is already written, maintains the secret hope that harmony of thought and mind may open paths different from those already assigned. I sincerely wish you a different incarnation from the one you foresaw. At least I hope it may be so.

I am, believe me, your

XAVIER JANATA MONROY

Vecchiano, 18 April 1985

Dear Mr Janata Monroy,
Your letter touched me deeply. It demands a reply, a reply that I fear will be considerably inferior to the one your letter postulates. First of all may I thank you for allowing me to use part of your name for a character in my book; and furthermore for not taking offence at the novelistic portrayal of the theosopher of Madras for which you provided the inspiration. Writers are not to be trusted even when claiming to practise the most rigorous realism: as far as I am concerned, therefore, you should treat me with the maximum distrust.

You confer on my little book, and hence on the vision of the world which emerges from it, a religious profundity and a philosophical complexity which unfortunately I do not believe I possess. But, as the poet we both know says, 'everything is worth the trouble if the spirit be not mean.' So that even my little book is worth the trouble, not so much for itself, but for what a broad spirit may read into it.

Still, books, as you know, are almost always bigger than ourselves. To speak of the person who wrote that book, I am obliged, in spite of myself, to descend to the anecdotal (I wouldn't dare to say biographical), which in my case is banal and low caste. The evening we made each other's acquaintance in the Theosophical Society, I had just survived a curious adventure. Many things had happened to me in Madras: I had had the good fortune to meet a number of people and to meditate on various strange stories. But what happened to me had to do with me alone. Thanks to the complicity of a temple guard, I had managed to get inside the compound of the Temple of Shiva the Destroyer, which, as you know, is strictly forbidden to non-Hindus, my precise intention being to photograph the altars. Since you appreciate the meaning I attribute to photography, you will realise that this amounted to a double sacrilege, perhaps even a challenge, since Shiva the Destroyer is identified with Death and with Time, is the *Bhoirava*, the Terror, and manifests himself in sixty-four forms which the temple of Madras illustrates and which I wanted to photograph for myself. It was two in the afternoon, when the temple shuts its gates for siesta, so that the place was entirely deserted with the exception of a few lepers who sleep there and who paid not the slightest attention. I know this will arouse a profound sense of disapproval on your part, but I do not want to lie. The heat was oppressive, the big monsoon had only just finished and the compound was full of stagnant puddles. Swarms of flies and insects wandered about in the air and the stench of excrement from the cows was unbearable. Opposite the altars to Shiva the traitor, beyond the troughs for the ablutions, is a small wall for votive offerings. I climbed upon it and began to take my photos. At that moment a piece of the wall I was standing on, being old and sodden with rain, collapsed. Of course I am giving you a 'pragmatic' explanation of what happened, since considered from another point of view the affair could have another explanation. In any event, when the wall crumbled I fell, skinning my right leg. A few hours later, when I'd got back to my hotel, the scratches had developed into an incredible swelling. It was only the following morning though, that I decided to go to the doctor, partly because I hadn't had myself vaccinated at all before coming to India and I was afraid I might have got infected by tetanus – certainly my leg showed every sign that that was what it was. To my considerable amazement, the doctor refused to give me an antitetanus shot. He said it was superfluous since, as he said, tetanus runs its course much faster in India than in Europe, and, 'if it were tetanus you would already be dead.' It was just 'a simple infection', he said, and all I needed was some streptomycin. He seemed quite surprised that I hadn't been infected by tetanus, but evidently, he concluded, one occasionally came across Europeans who had a natural resistance.

I'm sure you will find my story ridiculous, but it's the story I have to tell. As far as your gnostic interpretation of my *Nocturne*, or rather of its conclusion, is concerned, allow me to insist in all sincerity that I am not familiar with the Mandala and that my knowledge of Hindu philosophy is vague and very approximate, consisting as it does in the summary found in a tourist guide and in a pocket paperback I picked up at the airport called *L'Induisme* (part of the 'Que sais-je?' series). As regards the question of the mirror, I started doing some hurried research only after getting your letter. For help I went to the books of a serious scholar, Professor Grazia Marchianò, and am finding it hard work to grasp the basics of a philosophy of which I am woefully ignorant.

Finally I must say my own feeling is that on the most immediate level my *Nocturne* reflects a spiritual state which is far less profound than you so generously suppose. Private problems, of which I will spare you the tedious details, and then of course the business of finding myself in a continent so remote from my own world, had provoked an extremely strong sense of alienation towards everything: so much so that I no longer knew why I was there, what the point of my journey was, what sense there was in what I was doing or in what I myself might be. It was out of this alienation, perhaps, that my book sprang. In short, a misunderstanding. Evidently misunderstandings suit me. In confirmation of which allow me to send you this most recent book of mine, published a few days ago. You know Italian very well and may wish to take a look at it.

I am, believe me, your

ANTONIO TABUCCHI

Madras, 13 June 1985

Dear Mr Tabucchi,

My thanks for your letter and gift. I have just finished *Little Misunderstandings of No Importance* and your other book of short stories, *Reverse Side*, which you were generous enough to enclose. You did well, since the two complement each other and this made reading them more pleasant.

I am perfectly well aware that my letter caused you some embarrassment, just as I am also aware that you, for reasons of your own, wish to elude the gnostic interpretations that I gave of your books and which you, as I said, deny. As I mentioned in my first letter, Europeans visiting India can usually be divided into two categories:

those who believe they have discovered transcendence and those who profess the most radical secularism. I fear that despite your search for a third way, you do fall into these categories.

Forgive me my insistence. Even the philosophical position (may I so define it?) which you call 'Misunderstanding' corresponds, albeit dressed up in western culture (the Baroque), to the ancient Hindu precept that the misunderstanding (the error of life) is equivalent to an initiatory journey around the illusion of the real, that is around human life on earth. Everything is identical, as we say; and it seems to me that you affirm the same thing, even if you do so from a position of scepticism (are you by any chance considered a pessimist?). But I would like to abandon my culture for a moment and draw on yours instead. Perhaps you will remember Epimenides' paradox which goes more or less like this: 'The phrase that follows this is false: the phrase that precedes this is true'. As you will have noticed the two halves of the saying are mirrors of each other. Dusting off this paradox, an American mathematician, Richard Hoffstadter, author of a paper on Gödel's theorem, has recently called into question the whole Aristotelian–Cartesian logical dichotomy on which your culture is based and according to which every statement must be either true or false. This statement in fact can be simultaneously both true and false; and this because it refers to itself in the negative: it is a snake biting its own tail, or, to quote Hoffstadter's definition, 'a strange loop'.

Life too is a strange loop. We are back to Hinduism again. Do you at least agree on this much, Mr Tabucchi?

I am, believe me, your

XAVIER JANATA MONROY

Vecchiano, 10 July 1985

Dear Mr Janata Monroy,

As usual your letter has obliged me to make a rapid and I fear superficial attempt to assimilate some culture. I only managed to track down something about the American mathematician you mention in one Italian periodical, a column written from the USA by journalist Sandro Stille. The article was very interesting and I have promised myself to look into the matter more deeply. I do not, however, know much about mathematical logic, nor perhaps about any kind of logic; indeed I believe I am the most illogical person I know, and hence I don't imagine I will make much progress in studies of this variety. Perhaps, as you say, life really is 'a strange loop'. It seems fair that each of us should understand this expression in the cultural context that best suits him.

But allow me to give you a piece of advice. Don't believe too readily in what writers say: they lie (tell lies) almost all the time. A novelist who writes in Spanish and who perhaps you are familiar with, Mario Vargas Llosa, has said that writing a story is a performance not unlike a strip-tease. Just as the girl undresses under an immodest spotlight revealing her secret charms, so the writer lays bare his intimate life to the public through his stories. Of course there are differences. What the writer reveals are not, like the uninhibited girl, his secret charms, but rather the spectres that haunt him, the ugliest part of himself: his regrets, his guilt and his resentments. Another difference is that while in her performance the girl starts off dressed and ends up naked, in the case of the story the trajectory is inverted: the writer starts off naked and ends up dressed. Perhaps we writers are simply *afraid*. By all means consider us as cowards and leave us to our private guilt, our private ghosts. The rest is clouds.

Yours

ANTONIO TABUCCHI

The Battle of San Romano

I would have liked to talk to you about the sky over Castile. The blue and the swift billowing clouds driven by the upland wind, and the monastery of Santa Maria de Huerta, on the road to Madrid, where I arrived one late spring afternoon to find Orson Welles shooting *Falstaff*, and it seemed to me the most natural thing in the world to come across that big bearded man with a cigar in his mouth, wearing a waistcoat and sitting on a stool in the Cistercian cloister. To tell you: look, that's what I was like then, all those years ago, I liked Spain, *Hills like White Elephants*, it was like pushing aside the cork curtain of a small rather dirty tavern and walking straight into a book by Hemingway, that was the door to life, it smacked of literature, like a page from *Fiesta*. It was a feast day, a holiday, I wasn't the person I am now, I still had the innocent lightness of someone who is waiting for things to happen; I could still take risks, write those stories, like *Dinner with Federico*, describing the limbo of adolescence, lazy afternoons, cicadas: small beer then, but it would take some courage now.

I was listening to a poet reading his poetry; 'my

Southern Cross, my Hesperus,' and he was full of tenderness for a woman made of poetry, who in the end was himself. I sensed that he really did love this woman, because he loved her in the most authentic way possible, he loved himself in her, that is the real secret and in its own way a form of innocence, and I said to myself: too late.

Nice place, the hotel, with blackened mirrors and ornamented picture frames, neoclassical columns made of wood, a discreet carefully selected audience of the kind one finds late evenings in luxury hotels, and me there listening with my heart beating, full of remorse and shame.

Why did he have this courage when I didn't, I wondered. What is this quality? Poetry, unawareness, awareness, or what? And then I saw this patient vehicle which has been transporting us for thousands of years. In a tray of food on the sideboard was an orange, our teacher used to say to us: look children, this is the world, that's how it's made, like an orange. The image floated up suddenly from the well of memory, and I looked on the surface of that orange for the long roads of Castile, and for a small car driving fast, thinking it could get into life through the little cork curtain of a page of Hemingway, and instead all I saw was orange peel, it had disappeared entirely from the fruit's surface. The poet read his fine poem with a fine, polished voice, I was on the point of tears, but not because of what he was saying (or rather, only partly because of that); no, it was me, it was because I couldn't find the road of that afternoon on the orange, the afternoon I saw Orson Welles, the afternoon I would have liked to talk to you about. So then I went up to my room to look at the enlargements I'd brought with me from the dark room. I'd broken down the painting piece by piece, dividing it into a fine grid, and I'd photographed every little square of the grid; it will be a long, exacting job requiring patience, interminable evenings with lens and lamp. Blown up by the enlargement process the surface of the frame is an epidermis full of wrinkles and scars, it almost makes you feel sorry for it, you see it was once a living organism, and now here it is in front of me like a corpse and I anatomise it to give it a sense it has lost with the passage of time, and which perhaps is not the original sense, the same way I try to give meaning to that afternoon on the road to Madrid, and I know the sense I'm giving it is different, because it had its real sense only then, in that moment, when I didn't know what sense it had, and now when I give it a sense made up of youth, prints of Spain and novels of Hemingway, it's just the interpretation of the person I am now: after its fashion a fake.

This story, whose first person narrator must of course be taken to be a fictional character, owes much to the observations of two art historians apropos of two panels of Paolo Uccello's triptych, *The Battle of San Romano*, one of which is in the National Gallery, the other in the Louvre. Of the first, which shows Niccolò da Tolentino leading the Florentines, P. Francastel (*Peinture et société*, Lyon 1951) notes, upon analysing the spatial perspective, that Paolo Uccello simultaneously uses different perspectives, amongst them one elusive perspective close up and one 'compartmentalised' perspective in the background. The panel in the Louvre, which shows the part played by Micheletto da Cotignola, attracted the attention of A. Parronchi (*Studi sulla dolce prospettiva*, Milan 1964), again in response to problems of perspective. Parronchi examines the pictorial use of the silver leaves of the breastplates, and concludes that it is these which give the impression of reflections and of a multiplication of images. Basically the panel in the Louvre would seem to offer a way of playing with perspective already posited in Vitelione's *Perspectiva*; a method by which 'it is possible to arrange the mirror in such a way that the viewer sees in the air, outside the mirror, the image of something that is not within his field of vision'. In this way Paolo Uccello's panel would appear to offer a representation not of real beings, but of ghosts.

The only other thing I need say is that the author of this letter is writing to a female character.

Story of a Non-Existent Story

I have a non-existent novel whose story I would like to tell. The novel was called *Letters to Captain Nemo*, a title later altered to *No one behind the Door*. I wrote it in 1977, I think, in two weeks of rough seclusion and rapture in a little village near Siena. I'm not sure what inspired me: partly memories, which in my mind are almost always mixed up with fantasy and as a result not very reliable; partly the urgency of fiction itself which always carries a certain weight; and partly loneliness, which is often the writer's company. Without thinking much about it, I turned the story into a novel (a long short-story) and sent it to a publisher, who found it perhaps rather too allusive, and a little elusive, and then from the point of view of a publisher, not very accessible or decipherable. I think he was right. To be quite frank I don't know what its value in literary terms may or may not have been. I left it to settle for a while in a drawer, since I feel that obscurity and forgetfulness improve a story. Maybe I really did forget it. I came across it again a few years later and finding it made a strange impression on me. It rose quite suddenly from the

231

darkness of a dresser, from beneath stacks of paper, like a submarine rising from obscure depths. I saw an obvious metaphor in this, a message almost (the novel was partly about a submarine); and as though in justification, or expiation (it is strange how novels can bring on guilt complexes), I felt the need to add a concluding note, the only thing that now remains of the whole and which still bears the title: *Beyond the End*. This would have been the winter of 1979, I think. I made a few small changes to the novel, then entrusted it to a publisher of a variety I thought might be more suitable for a difficult book like this. My choice turned out to be right, agreement was quickly reached and I promised delivery for the following autumn. Except that during the summer holidays I took the typescript with me in my suitcase. It had been alone for a long time and I felt it needed company. I read it again towards the end of August. I was by the Atlantic in an old house inhabited by wind and ghosts. These were not my ghosts, but real ghosts: pitiful presences which it took only the smallest amount of sensitivity or receptiveness to become aware of. And then I was particularly sensitive at the time because I knew the history of the house well and likewise the people who had lived there: by one of life's inexplicable coincidences my own life and theirs had become mixed up together. Meanwhile September had come around bringing those violent sea storms that usher in the equinox; sometimes the house would be blacked out, the trees in the big garden waved their restless branches, and all night long the corridors echoed with the groans of ageing woodwork. Occasionally friends would come to dinner, the headlamps of their cars carving white swathes in the darkness. In front of the house was a cliff with a fearful drop straight into the seething waves. I was alone, I knew that for certain, and in the loneliness of existence the restless presences of the ghosts try to make contact. But real conversations are impossible, you have to make do with bizarre, untranslatable codes, stratagems invented *ad hoc*. I could think of nothing better than to rely on a flashing light. There was a lighthouse on the other side of the bay. It sent out two beams and had four different time gaps. Using combinations of these variables I invented a mental language that was very approximate but good enough for basic conversation. Some nights I would suffer from insomnia. The old house had a big terrace and I would spend the night talking to the lighthouse, using it, that is, to transmit my messages, or to receive messages, depending on the situation, the whole exchange being orchestrated by myself, of course. But some things are easier than one imagines; for example, all you have to do is think: tonight I'm transmitting; or: tonight I'm receiving. And you're set.

I received many stories during those nights. I confess to transmitting very little. Most of the time I spent listening. Those presences were eager

233

to talk and I sat and listened to their stories, trying to decipher communications which were often subject to interference, obscure and full of gaps. They were unhappy stories for the most part, that much I sensed quite clearly. Thus, amid those silent dialogues, the autumn equinox came round. That day the sea was whipped up into a storm. I heard it thundering away from dawn on. In the afternoon an enormous force convulsed its bowels. Come evening, thick clouds had descended on the horizon and communication with my ghosts was lost. I went to the cliffs around two in the morning, having waited for the beam of the lighthouse in vain. The ocean was howling quite unbearably, as if full of voices and laments. I took my novel with me and consigned it to the wind page by page. I don't know if it was a tribute, a homage, a sacrifice or a penance.

Years have gone by, and now that story surfaces again from the obscurity of other dressers, other depths. I see it in black and white, the way I see things in dreams usually. Or in faded, extremely tenuous colours; and with a light mist all around, a thin veil that blurs and softens the edges. The screen it is projected on is the night sky of an Atlantic coast in front of an old house called São José da Guia. To those old walls, which no longer exist as I knew them, and to everybody who knew the house before I did and lived there, I duly dedicate this non-existent novel.

The Translation

It's a splendid day, you can be sure of that, indeed I'd say it was a summer's day, you can't mistake summer, I'm telling you, and I'm an expert. You want to know how I knew? Oh, well, it's easy really, how can I put it?, all you have to do is look at that yellow. What do I mean by that? Okay, now listen carefully, you know what yellow is? Yes, yellow, and when I say yellow I really do mean yellow, not red or white, but real yellow, precisely, yellow. That yellow over there on the right, that star-shaped patch of yellow opening across the countryside as if it were a leaf, a glow, something like that, of grass dried out by the heat, am I making myself clear?

That house looks as if it's right on top of the yellow, as if it were held up by yellow. It's strange one can only see a bit of it, just a part, I'd like to know more, I wonder who lives there, maybe that woman crossing the little bridge. It would be interesting to know where she's going, maybe she's following the gig, or perhaps it's a barouche, you can see it there near the two poplars in the background, on the left-hand side. She could be a widow, she's wearing black. And then she

235

has a black umbrella too. Though she's using that to keep off the sun, because as I said, it's summer, no doubt about it. But now I'd like to talk about that bridge — that delicate little bridge — it's so graceful, all made of bricks, the supports go as far as the middle of the canal. You know what I think? Its grace has to do with that clever contrivance of wood and ropes that covers it, like the scaffolding of a cantilever. It looks like a toy for an intelligent child, you know those children who look like little grown-ups and are always playing with Meccano and things like that, you used to see them in respectable families, maybe not so much now, but you've got the idea. But it's all an illusion, because the way I see it that graceful little bridge apparently meant to open considerately to let the boats on the canal go through, is really a very nasty trap. The old woman doesn't know, poor thing, she's got no idea at all, but now she's going to take another step and it'll be a fatal one, believe me, she's sure to put her foot on the treacherous mechanism, there'll be a soundless click, the ropes will tighten, the beams suspended cantilever fashion will close like jaws and she'll be caught inside like a mouse, if things go well that is, because in a worst-case scenario all the bars that connect the beams, those poles there, rather sinister if you think about it, will snap together, one right against the other with not a millimetre between and, wham, she'll be crushed flat as a pancake. The man driving the gig doesn't even realise, maybe he's deaf into the bargain, and then the woman's nothing to him, believe me, he's got other things to think about, if he's a farmer he'll be thinking of his vineyards, farmers never think about anything but the soil, they're pretty self-centred, for them the world ends along with their patch of ground; or if he's a vet, because he could be a vet too, he'll be thinking about some sick cow in the farm which must be back there somewhere, even if you can't see it, cows are more important than people for vets, everybody has his work in this world, what do you expect, and the others had better look out for themselves.

I'm sorry you still haven't understood, but if you make an effort I'm sure you'll get there, you're a smart person and it doesn't take much to work it out, or rather, maybe it does take a bit, but I think I've given you details enough; I'll repeat, probably all you have to do is connect together the pieces I've given you, in any event, look, the museum is about to close, see the custodian making signs to us, I can't bear these custodians, they give themselves such airs, really, but if you want let's come back tomorrow, in the end you don't have that much to do either, do you? and then Impressionism is charming, ah these Impressionists, so full of light, of colour, you almost get a smell of lavender from their paintings, oh yes, Provence . . . I've always had a soft spot for these landscapes, don't forget your stick, otherwise you'll get run over by some car or other, you put it down there, to the right, a bit further, to the right, you're nearly there, remember, three paces to our left there's a step.

Happy People

'I'm afraid we're going to get bad weather this evening,' said the girl and she pointed to a curtain of clouds on the horizon. She was skinny and angular, her hands moving jerkily, and she had her hair done up in a little ponytail. The terrace of the small restaurant looked out over the sea. To the right, beyond the screen of jasmine which climbed up to form a pergola, you could glimpse a little courtyard full of bric-à-brac, cases of empty bottles, a few broken chairs. To the left was a small ironwork gate, beneath which gleamed the little stairway carved into the sheer rock face. The waiter arrived with a tray of steaming shellfish. He was a little man with slicked-back hair and a shy manner. He put the tray down on the table and made a slight bow. On his right arm he carried a dirty napkin.

'I like this country,' said the girl to the man sitting opposite, 'the people are simple and kind.'

The man didn't answer; he unfolded his napkin, tucking it into the collar of his shirt, but then registered the girl's disapproving look at once and rearranged it on his knees. 'I don't like it,' he answered, 'I don't understand the

239

language. And then it's too hot. And then I don't like southern countries.'

The man was about sixtyish, with a square face and thick eyebrows. But his mouth was pink and moist, with something soft about it.

The girl shrugged her shoulders. She seemed visibly annoyed, as if his confession contrasted somehow with her own candour. 'You're not being fair,' she said, 'they've paid for everything, the trip, the hotel, they couldn't have treated you with more respect.'

He waved his hand in a gesture of indifference. 'I didn't come for their country, I came for the conference. They treat me with great respect and I show mine by being here, so we're quits.' He concentrated on cracking open his lobster, making it plain there was nothing else to say about the matter. A small gust of wind blew away the paper napkin covering the bread-basket. The sea was getting choppy and was deep deep blue.

The girl seemed put out, but maybe it was just a show. When she finally spoke it was in a tone of faint resentment, but with a hint of reconciliation too. 'You didn't even tell me what you'll be talking about, it's as if you wanted to keep me in the dark about everything, which isn't fair I don't think.'

He had finally managed to overcome the resistance of his lobster and was now dipping the meat in mayonnaise. His face brightened and in a single breath, like a schoolboy parroting a lesson, he said: 'Structures and Distortions in Middle Latin and Vulgar Texts of the Pays d'Oc.'

The girl gulped, as if her food had gone down the wrong way, and she began to laugh. She laughed uncontrollably, covering her mouth with her napkin. 'Oh dear,' she hiccupped, 'oh dear!'

He started to laugh too, but stopped himself because he wasn't sure whether it was best for him to join in her outburst of hilarity or not. 'Explain,' he asked, when she had calmed down.

'Nothing,' the girl said, between intermittent giggles. 'It just occurred to me that you're rather better suited to the vulgar than the Middle Latin, that's all.'

He shook his head in fake pity, but you could see deep down he was flattered. 'In any event we can begin the lesson now; so listen carefully.' He held up a thumb and said: 'Point number one: you have to study the minor authors, it's the minor authors will make your career, all the greats have already been studied.' He raised another finger. 'Point number two: make the bibliography as long as you possibly can, taking care to disagree with scholars who are dead.' He raised yet another finger. 'Point number three: no fanciful methodologies, I know they're in fashion now, but they'll sink without a trace, stay with the straightforward and tradi-tional.' She was listening carefully, concentrating hard. Perhaps the sketch of a timid objection was forming on her face, because he felt the need to offer an example. 'Think of that French specialist who came to talk about Racine and all Phaedra's complexes,' he said. 'A normal person, would you say?'

'What? Phaedra?' asked the girl, as though thinking of something else.

'The French specialist,' he said patiently.

The girl didn't answer.

'Quite,' he said. 'These days critics are in the habit of unloading their own neuroses onto literary texts. I had the courage to say as much and you saw how outraged everybody was.' He opened the menu and set about a careful choice of dessert. 'Psychoanalysis was the invention of a madman,' he concluded, 'everybody knows that, but you try saying it out loud.'

The girl looked absent-mindedly at the sea. She had a resigned expression and was almost pretty. 'So what next?' she asked, still speaking as though her mind were elsewhere.

'I'll tell you that later,' said the man. 'Right now I want to say something else. You know what's positive about us, our winning card? Do you? It's that we're normal people, that's what.' He finally settled on a dessert and waved to the waiter. 'And now I'll tell you what next,' he went on. 'What's next is, you apply for the place right now.'

'But we'll have your philologist friend against us,' she objected.

'Oh, him,' exclaimed the man. 'He'll keep quiet he will, or rather, he'll be on our side, you'll see.' He left a pause that was full of mystery.

'When he walks down the corridor with his pipe and hair blowing about, you'd think he was God the Father himself,' she said. 'He can't bear me, he doesn't even say hello.'

'He'll learn to say hello, sweetie.'

'I told you not to call me sweetie, it brings me out in a rash.'

'In any event he'll learn to say hello,' he interrupted. He smiled with a sly look and poured himself some wine. He was doing it on purpose to increase the mystery and wanted it to be obvious he was doing it on purpose. 'I know all sorts of little things about him,' he finally said, letting a glimmer of light into the darkness.

'Tell me about them.'

'Oh, little things,' he muttered with affected casualness, 'certain escapades, old friendships with people in this country when it was not exactly a paragon of democracy. If I was a novelist I could write a story about it.'

'Oh come on,' she said, 'I don't believe it. He's always in the front row when it comes to petitions and meetings, he's left-wing.'

The man seemed to think over the adjective she'd used: 'Left-handed rather,' he concluded.

The girl laughed, shaking her head, which made her ponytail bob from side to side. 'In any event, we'll need support from someone from another university,' she said, 'we can't keep everything in the family.'

'I've thought of that too.'

'You think of everything, do you?'

'In all modesty . . .'

'Who?'

'No names.'

He smiled affably, took the girl's hand and

assumed a paternal manner. 'Listen carefully, you have to analyse people's motives, and that's just what I do. Everybody runs a mile from him, have you ever asked yourself why?'

The girl shook her head and he made a vague, mysterious gesture. 'There must be a reason,' he said.

'I've got a reason of my own,' she said. 'I'm pregnant.'

'Don't be stupid,' said the man with a cutting smile.

'Don't be stupid yourself,' the girl answered sharply.

The man had frozen with a slice of pineapple just an inch from his mouth; his face betrayed the surprise of someone who has recognised the truth.

'Since when?'

'Two months.'

'Why wait till now to tell me?'

'Because I didn't feel like it before,' she said firmly. She made a broad gesture which included the sea, the sky and the waiter who was arriving with the coffee. 'If it's a girl I'm going to call her Felicity,' she said with conviction.

The man slipped the pineapple into his mouth and swallowed in haste. 'A bit too passé and sentimental for my taste.'

'Okay, so Allegra, Joy, Serena, Hope, Letitia, Hilary, as you will. I don't care what you say, I think names have an influence on a person's character, hear yourself called Hilary all the time and you begin to feel a bit hilarious, you laugh. I want a cheerful child.'

The man didn't answer. He turned to the waiter hovering patiently at a distance and made as if to write on his hand. The waiter understood and went into the restaurant to prepare the bill. There was a curtain of metal beads over the door which tinkled every time someone went in. The girl stood up and took hold of the man's hand, pulling him up.

'Come on, come and look at the sea, don't play the crotchety old fogy, this is the best day of your life.'

The man got up a little unwillingly, letting himself be pulled. The girl put her arm round his waist, pushing him on. 'It's you who looks pregnant,' she said, 'about six months if you ask me.' She let out a ringing laugh and hopped like a little bird. They leaned on the wooden parapet. There were some agave plants in the small unkept piece of ground in front of the terrace and lots of wild flowers. The man took a cigarette from his pocket and slipped it between his lips. 'Oh God,' she said, 'not that unbearable stink again, it'll be the first thing I'll cut out of our life.'

'You just try,' he said with a sly look.

She held him tight against her, stroking his cheek with her head. 'This restaurant is delightful.'

The man patted his stomach. His expression was one of satisfaction and self-assurance. 'You have to know how to take life,' he answered.

The Archives of Macao

'Listen, my good man, your father has cancer of the pharynx, I can't leave the conference to operate on him tomorrow, I've invited half Italy, do you understand? And then, with what he's got a week isn't going to make much difference.'

'Actually our doctor says the operation should be done immediately, because it's a type of cancer that spreads extremely quickly.'

'Oh really, immediately indeed? And what am I supposed to say to the people coming to the conference, that I have to operate tomorrow and the conference is being postponed? Listen, your father will do what everybody else does, wait until the conference is finished.'

'You listen to me, Professor Piragine, I don't give a damn about your conference, I want my father to be operated immediately, and any others too, if they're urgent.'

'I have no intention of discussing the schedule of my operating theatre with you. This is the University of Pisa and I am not just a doctor, I have well-defined teaching duties as well. I'm not going to put up with you telling me what I have to do. I can't operate on your father until next week; if that's not good enough, have the patient discharged and find another hospital. It goes without saying that the responsibility will be yours. Goodbye.'

The voice of the hostess invited the passengers to buckle their safety belts and extinguish their cigarettes, the stopover would last about forty minutes for refuelling and cleaning. And as through the window one began to see the lights of Bombay and a little later the blue lights of the runway, just then – it must have been due to the slight bump as the plane touched down, sometimes these things do spark off associations of ideas – I found myself on your scooter. You were driving with your arms out wide, because in those days the scooters used to have wide handlebars, and I was watching your scarf blowing in the wind. The fringe was tickling me and I wanted to scratch my nose but I was afraid of falling. It was 1956, I'm sure of that, because you bought the scooter as a celebration the same day I turned thirteen. I tapped two fingers on your shoulder, to ask you to slow down, and you turned smiling, and as you turned the scarf slipped from your neck, very slowly, as if every movement of objects in space had been put into slow motion, and I saw that beneath the scarf you had a horrible wound slicing across your throat from one side to the other, so wide and open I could see the muscle tissue, the blood vessels, the carotid artery, the pharynx, but you didn't know you had the wound and you smiled unaware, and in fact you didn't have it, it was me seeing it there, it's strange how one sometimes finds oneself superimposing one memory over another, that was what I was doing, I was remembering how you were in 1956 and then adding the last image you were to leave me, almost thirty years later.

I appreciate one shouldn't write to the dead, but you know perfectly well that sometimes writing to the dead is an excuse, it's an elementary Freudian truth, because it's the quickest way of writing to oneself, and so forgive me, I am writing to myself, even though perhaps I am writing to the memory of you I keep inside me, the mark you left inside me, and hence in a certain sense I really am writing to you – but no, perhaps this too is an excuse, the truth is I am writing to no one but myself: even my memory of you, that mark you left inside me, is exclusively my business, you are nowhere and in nothing, there's just me, sitting here on a seat in this jumbo heading for Hong Kong and imagining I'm riding on a scooter, I thought I was on a scooter, I knew perfectly well I was flying on a plane that was taking me to Hong Kong from where I'll then take a boat to Macao, except that I was riding on a scooter, it was my thirteenth birthday, you were driving with your scarf round your neck and I was going to Macao by scooter. And without turning round, the fringe of your scarf in the wind tickling me, you shouted: To Macao? What on

248

earth are you going to Macao for? And I said: I'm going to look for some documents in the archives there, there's a municipal archive, and then the archive of an old school too, I'm going to look for some papers, some letters maybe, I'm not sure, basically some manuscripts of a symbolist poet, a strange man who lived in Macao for thirty-five years, he was an opium addict, he died in 1926, a Portuguese, called Camilo Pessanha, the family was originally from Genoa, his ancestor, a certain Pezagno, was in the service of the Portuguese king in 1300. He was a poet, he only wrote one little book of poems, *Clepsydra*, listen to this line: 'The wild roses have bloomed by mistake.' And you asked me: 'You think that makes any sense?'

Last Invitation

For the solitary traveller, admittedly rare but perhaps not implausible, who cannot resign himself to the lukewarm, standardised forms of hospitalised death which the modern state guarantees and who, what's more, is terrorised at the thought of the hurried and impersonal treatment to which his unique body will be subjected during the obsequies, Lisbon still offers an admirable range of options for a noble suicide, together with the most decorous, solemn, zealous, polite and above all cheap organisations for dealing with what a successful suicide inevitably leaves behind it: the corpse.

Choosing a place suitable for a voluntary exit, and deciding on the manner of that exit, has become an almost hopeless undertaking these days, so much so that even the most eager are resigning themselves to natural forms of death, aided perhaps by the idea, now widespread in people's consciousness, that the atomic destruction of the planet, the Total Suicide, is just a question of time, and hence what's the point of taking so much trouble? This last idea is very much open to question, and if nothing else misleading in its cunning syllogism: first because it creates a connivance with Death and hence a sort of resignation to the so-called 'Inevitable' (a feeling necessarily alien to the exquisitely private act of suicide which can in no way be subjected to collectivist notions without its very essence being perverted); and second, even in the event of the Great Explosion, why on earth should this be considered a suicide, rather than a homicide inspired by destructive impulses towards others and the self carried out on a large scale and similar to those which inspired the wretched Nazis? And coercive in nature too, and hence in contrast with the inalienable nature of the act of suicide, which consists, as we know, in freedom of choice.

Furthermore it has to be said that while waiting for the Total Suicide, people are still dying, a fact I consider worthy of reflection. And dying not just in the traditional and ancient fashions, but also and to a great extent as a result of factors connected with those same diabolical traps which foreshadow the Total Suicide. Such little inventions, for the solemn reason, amongst many others, that the cathode tubes of our houses must be on and that we must thus supply them with energy, are daily distributing their doses of poison which being indiscriminate are, if we wish to cavil, democratic; in short, while insinuating the idea of the inevitable Total Suicide, these things are all the time carrying out a systematic, constant and I would even say progressive form of homicide. Thus the potential suicide who does not kill himself because he might just as well wait for the Total Suicide, does not reflect, poor sucker, that in the meantime he is absorbing radioactive strontium, cesium and other delights of that ilk, and that while postponing his departure he is quite possibly already nursing in liver, lungs or spleen, one of the innumerable forms of cancer that the above-mentioned elements so prodigally produce.

In indicating a place where one might still kill oneself with dignity, in complete liberty, and in ways esteemed by our ancestors and now apparently lost, one does not pretend to offer a public service (though it could be that), but to promote reflection, from a purely theoretical point of view, on a liberty: a hypothetical initiative practised upon ourselves which might be carried out without sinking to the more disheartening and vulgar stratagems to which the would-be suicide inevitably seems to be constrained in those countries defined as industrially advanced. (Obviously I am not referring to countries where problems of political, mental or physical survival exist and where suicide presents itself as a form of desperation and thus outside the realm of the kind of suicide here discussed which is based on freedom of choice.)

From this point of view Lisbon would seem to be a city of considerable resources.

The first confirmation comes upon consultation of the telephone directory, where the undertakers fill a good sixteen pages. Sixteen pages in the Yellow Pages are a lot, you will have to agree, especially if one considers that Lisbon is not an enormous city; it is a first and very telling indication of the number of companies operating in the area, the only problem being that one is spoilt for choice. A second consideration is that death, in Portugal, does not appear to belong, as it does in other countries, to that ambiguous area of reticence and 'shame'. There is nothing shameful about dying, and death is justly considered a necessary fact of life; hence the arrangements which have to do with death get the same attention as other useful services to the citizen, such as *Águas*, *Restaurantes*, *Transportes*, *Teatros* (I mention a few at random), all services of public utility which can be contacted by phone. In line with this reasoning, the undertakers of Lisbon do not shun advertising: and in the telephone directory they advertise most forthrightly, with show, with pomp, and undeniable charm. Sober or ornate, and using extremely pertinent slogans, they will often take out a whole page to illustrate their services.

Some of them appeal to tradition: '*Há mais de meio século serve meia Lisboa*' (has served half of Lisbon for more than half a century), boasts the advertisement of an undertaker based in Avenida Almirante Reis, and while the adjective *meio* referred to time seems to offer a purely historical piece of information, the *meia Lisboa* suggests something less statistically quantifiable, something warmer and more familiar; 'half of Lisbon', in this case, means a majority, almost all, with slight connotations of classlessness. The dead of every social class and level, the announcement implies, are looked after by this traditional and implacable undertaker. Other undertakers, on the contrary, stress efficiency and modernisation. '*Os únicos auto-fúnebres automáticos*' (the only automatic hearses), claims an agency which boasts four branches covering the whole city. Modernity and mechanisation are powerful attractions, but this advertisement is certainly playing on the customer's curiosity. What on earth might automisation mean when applied to hearses? Worth checking out.

Almost all the undertakers also stress their experience and serious professional approach. To get this over, their ads in the Yellow Pages are accompanied by the faces of the proprietors and their staff: the unambiguous faces of undertakers with years of honest and respectable work behind them. What matters here is reliability, competence and the division of labour. These people don't disguise the physiognomy of their profession; on the contrary, they display the stereotype with pride. They have sorrowful but shrewd faces, long sideburns and often dark beards, very carefully trimmed. Their shoulders slope a little, they have black jackets, black ties, and quite frequently glasses with heavy plastic frames. They know how to manage the business of death, that much is clear, that's what they've always done and they're proud of it. You can feel safe with undertakers like this.

But the most interesting advert for the potential customer comes from a discreet undertakers which stresses its *Serviço Permanente* and offers this copy line: '*Nos momentos difíceis a opção certa*' (the right choice at a difficult moment). Further down in the ad, after the reassuring guarantee that the company only uses *flores naturais*, we have another line: '*Faça do nosso serviço um bom serviço, preferindo-nos*' (make our service a good service by choosing us). To whom can these lines be directed if not to the interested party him or herself? The preferred target of this thoughtful undertaker is without doubt the man about to die. It is to *him* that the company wishes to talk, come to an understanding, achieve complicity. There is something of the conjugal in these bare and at the same time anodyne lines: they seem the quintessence of a contract, or a commonplace, they would be entirely plausible in the mouth of Emma Bovary's husband, in the evening in front of the fire. Or again in the mouths of any of us when we sit down to eat our dinner and set up a relationship of reciprocal connivance with what we call living.

Places to die, means of dying – they are so many and so varied one would need to write a whole treatise to cover them. I would rather leave the question up to the user, if only so as not to deprive suicide of that flair and creativity it ought to have. However, one can hardly avoid mentioning the means which, given the city's structure and topography, would seem to be Lisbon's chosen vocation: the leap. I appreciate that the void has always been a major attraction for spirits on the run. Even when he knows that the ground awaits him below, the man who chooses the void implies his refusal of fullness; he is terrified of the material world and desires to go the way of the Eternal Void, by falling for a few seconds through the physical void. Then the leap is also akin to flight; it involves a sort of rebellion against the human condition as biped; it tends towards space, towards vast distances, towards the horizon. Well then, when it comes to this noble form of suicide, Lisbon is certainly the location par excellence. Hilly, constantly changing, riddled with stairways, sudden terraces, holes, drops, spaces that open all at once before you, complete with historic places for Historic suicides (try the Aqueducto das Águas Livres, the Castle, the Tower of Belém), sophisticated places for Art Deco suicides (the Elevador de Santa Justa) and mechanical places for Constructivist suicides (the Ponte 25 de Abril), this beautiful city offers the eager candidate a range of jumps unrivalled by any other European city. But the spot which lends itself more than any other to the leap is without a doubt the Cristo Rei on the banks of the Tagus. Undeniably this Christ is an invitation writ in stone, a sculptor's hymn in praise of the leap, a suggestion, a symbol, perhaps an allegory. This Christ offers us the very image of the *plongeur*, his arms outspread on a spring-board from which he is ready to hurl himself. He

is not an impostor he is a companion, and that
brings a certain comfort. Beneath flows the
Tagus. Slow, calm, powerful. Ready to welcome
the body of the volunteer and carry him down to
the Atlantic, thus rendering superfluous even the
most solicitous attentions of Lisbon's undertakers.

For brevity's sake I shall say nothing of other
forms of suicide. But before I sign off, one at least,
out of a sense of duty to a whole culture, I must
mention. It is an unusual and subtle form, it takes
training, constancy, determination. It is death by
Saudade, originally a category of the spirit, but
also an attitude that you can learn if you really
want to. The Lisbon city council has always made
public benches available in appointed sites in the
city: the quays by the harbour, the belvederes, the
gardens which look out over the sea. Lots of
people sit on them. They sit silently, looking into
the distance. What are they doing? They are
practising *Saudade*. Try imitating them. Of
course it's a difficult road to take, the effects are
not immediate, sometimes you may have to be
willing to wait many years. But death, as we all
know, is that too.